Immanuel

W9-CPE-562

Kewaunee

Grace Lutheran School
415 N. 6th Place
Lowell, AR 72745
(479) 659-5999

BOOKS BY CHARLENE JOY TALBOT

A Home With Aunt Florry
The Great Rat Island Adventure
An Orphan for Nebraska
The Sodbuster Venture

The
Sodbuster
Venture

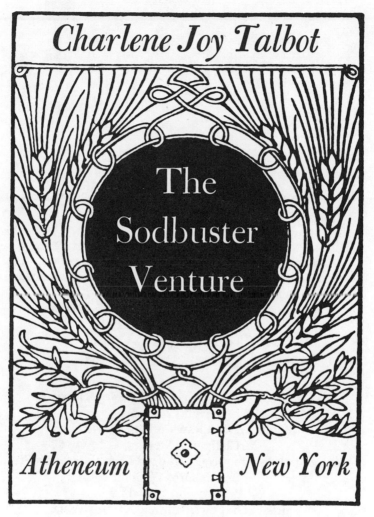

Charlene Joy Talbot

The
Sodbuster
Venture

Atheneum   New York

·1982·

LIBRARY OF CONGRESS CATALOGING IN PUBLICATION DATA

Talbot, Charlene Joy.
The sodbuster venture.

SUMMARY: Following a dying man's last request,
thirteen-year-old Maud helps the man's fiancé homestead
his claim on the Kansas prairie in 1870.
[1. Frontier and pioneer life—Kansas—Fiction.
2. Kansas—Fiction]   I. Title.
PZ7.T1418So   [Fic]   81-8051
ISBN 0-689-30893-0   AACR2

Published simultaneously in Canada by
McClelland & Stewart, Ltd.
Composition by American–Stratford Graphic Services, Inc.,
Brattleboro, Vermont
Printed and bound by
Fairfield Graphics, Fairfield, Pennsylvania
Designed by M. M. Ahern
First Edition

For Joann Dilello

Contents

The
Sodbuster
Venture

1
A
Death

MAUD MCPHERSON balanced the bucket of water on the well curb and shaded her eyes with her hand. She stared across the prairie, hoping to see two riders. Except for the line of treetops marking the fold of Dry Creek, she saw nothing but waving grass, shimmering under the July sun.

Maud carried the water into the house and set the bucket by the door. Her eyes adjusted to the dark, hot room. The man on the bed was awake.

"Do you want a drink, Mr. Nelson?" she asked him.

He nodded without speaking. Every time he tried to talk now, the dreadful coughing began. She carried half a dipperful of cool water to the bedside. His eyes asked a question.

"No one in sight," she told him.

It was time to start peeling potatoes for dinner. Maud wondered if she ought to cook enough so she could offer dinner to the Coddingtons when they came, but she decided not to. Carrying a message to the doctor hadn't put them to any trouble. They had been going to town anyway. And Mr. Nelson was too sick for company.

Maud took the pan of potatoes and Mr. Nelson's bowie knife and sat on the doorstep to peel them. She was almost finished when two riders appeared out of a draw, perhaps a mile away, their dark shapes made wavery by the shimmering heat.

"They're coming," she told Mr. Nelson. She built a quick brush fire in the little iron stove and put the kettle on. She would offer them tea, no more. She'd cook the potatoes after they'd gone.

She waited in the dooryard—a strong, capable thirteen-year-old in a faded gray dress. Her red hair needed rebraiding. Her face, hands, and bare feet were nearly solid with freckles. She could only hope that—like the ugly duckling—she'd grow up beautiful, but the change had to be soon; she was growing up fast.

The men rode in, looking the worse for wear after their Saturday night spree in Abilene. Their wrinkled shirts were dark with sweat, their beards dusty, their eyes bloodshot. Neither lifted his hat, which was all right with Maud. She didn't expect fancy manners from Jake or Eph Coddington.

"Is the doctor coming?" she demanded.

"Yep." Jake, the older brother swung down from his horse. "Soon as he finishes patching up a couple of cowboys."

"Yeah," Eph chimed in, his dull eyes suddenly alight. "They was shooting all over the place!"

"Nelson still alive?" Jake asked.

"Of course!" Maud exclaimed, hoping Jake's question hadn't been heard inside the sod house.

The men led their horses to the hollowed-out cottonwood log that was the water trough. It was nearly dry.

"Eph, draw some water," Jake ordered.

Eph slouched to the well.

"Do you want a cup of tea?" Maud asked.

"On a day like this?" Jake scoffed. "Just give me a drink of water. Unless there's coffee?"

Maud shook her head. "We're out."

The drinking can was hanging from the well post. Jake drank first and then Eph. They did everything that way. Eph was turned twenty-one, but he wasn't bright. Jake told him what to do and he did it. Mr. Nelson said that sooner or later Jake would tell him to do something against the law, and Eph would get caught. They were no-goods—the kind Mr. Nelson said you could find all over the plains, without even looking for. They were better than no neighbors at all, but not much.

Jake wiped his beard and turned toward the house. Maud followed anxiously, hoping he wouldn't get Mr. Nelson to talking. If Mr. Nelson tried to talk, he'd start to cough.

Jake sat on a nail keg. "Howdy, Silas. Had some excitement in town last night. Two Texans shooting each other up. Doc said he'll come out when he finishes digging for bullets."

The man on the bed seemed not to hear. His eyes were closed, his chest not moving.

Jake got up and motioned Maud outside. "He ain't got long," he said brutally. "Doc won't be no help."

Maud felt the pit of her stomach go empty. "He takes a nap this time of day," she said stoutly.

Jake shrugged. "He looks done up to me. Looks like you'll have to go back to your sister's. Less'n you want to keep house for Eph and me?" His grin showed tobacco-stained, crooked teeth.

Maud's blue eyes blazed. "He's going to get well! His sweetheart's coming tomorrow on the train."

"She'll be lucky to see him alive." Jake crossed the yard to his horse. Eph was already mounted. Jake sprang into the saddle, and they rode away.

Troubled, Maud crept into the house and stood looking down at the ailing man. Mr. Nelson had hired her to look after him when he got too sick to look after himself. Mr. Nelson was a gentleman. He treated Maud, young as she was, like a lady. Thanks to him she had been away from her sister's for two months, away from her sister's husband, who was coarse. Lately he'd begun looking at Maud in a way she didn't like.

The sick man did not move throughout the long afternoon. And the doctor did not come.

How many hours did it take to remove a few bullets, Maud wondered angrily. The cowboys deserved their wounds. But Silas Nelson didn't deserve to be sick. He had contracted lung disease in a Rebel prison. After the war, like a lot of other out-of-work soldiers, he'd come to Kansas to take up a homestead claim, hoping the dry air would cure him. Now his sweetheart was coming. He mustn't die.

Maud had cooked plenty of potatoes so she could fry some for the doctor. She fried bacon and ate it with the potatoes and drank a cup of tea.

The day seemed as timeless as the prairie itself. The sun crawled across the immense sky. Again and again she stared northwest, but the prairie was always empty. The day was Sunday, so her choice of occupation was limited.

At last she took Mr. Nelson's Bible from the shelf and sat in the doorway reading the fine print until it grew too dark. A full moon was rising; surely the doctor would still come.

She lit the kerosene lamp, carefully replacing the cracked glass chimney that Mr. Nelson had wired together.

The light roused him. She heard the straw mattress rustle and turned to find his eyes upon her. She offered him tea, and he nodded. She wondered if she ought to make some potato soup and feed it to him. It would be a relief to turn the nursing over to Miss Warren. He had asked Maud not to go back to her sister's but to stay and help Miss Warren get in the way of things.

When the tea was ready, she poured out a cupful and took it to the bed. He struggled to sit up, and she propped the folded comforter behind him.

"I want to talk to you," he said. Maud poured herself a cup of tea and sat on the nail keg.

"I may not last till Belle gets here," he said. Belle was Miss Warren. Miraculously he did not begin to cough. "I want you to convince her to stay anyway. Make her see what a fine future this country has, with the best farming and grazing land in America. If Belle moves fast, she can take over my claim. Tell her how it's the best quarter section around. She mustn't go back to her brother. She'll be better off here, even with the Coddingtons hanging around. There's good men out here, too. Back there she'll just wither. Tell her—" He started to cough. "Tell her I wish she'd try it for a year. Promise me you'll tell her that."

"I'll tell her." Maud spoke above his coughing.

"Promise me—*cough, cough*—you'll stay with her."

"I'll be glad to, if she wants me."

The rag he held to his mouth came away bright with blood. Oh, God, Maud prayed, let the doctor hurry!

He took another swallow of tea and handed her the cup. "You're a good girl, Maud," he whispered. He closed his eyes and lay back.

Maud repeated his message silently, over and over. He seemed to have no more to say. She wondered whether to remove the comforter so he could lie back.

"She'll be here any day." He spoke dreamily.

"Tomorrow, Mr. Nelson."

"What?"

"I said, she'll be here tomorrow. If you just hold out, everything will be fine, and you'll get well."

He turned his head to look at her. His eyes were feverish. "You promised—don't forget!"

Fear invaded the room. Maud stared into the dark outside the door, but there was nothing out there except the prairie night, with crickets and a faraway coyote.

"Cross my heart," Maud said.

Mr. Nelson's eyes closed; he seemed to be falling asleep.

Maud took up her piece bag and began sewing squares together. Sunday was as good as over. From time to time she went to look at him. His face above the black beard was almost as white as the sheet that covered him.

He died without her knowing. She only knew that one time when she looked at him his face was faintly damp. The next time his skin was gray and lifeless. Hesitantly she touched his forehead. It was cold.

Her hands flew to her mouth in fear, and then she thought of saying the Twenty-Third Psalm aloud. After that the night no longer seemed dreadful.

From somewhere she remembered that his arms ought to be crossed on his breast before the body grew cold. His eyes were already closed. She crossed the arms and pulled the sheet over his face. She sobbed once, but the event was too awesome for tears. She went and sat on the doorstep to wait for morning.

She must have fallen asleep, for suddenly a man was speaking to her, the lamplight shining on him and his horse. He was young and clean-shaven.

"I'm the doctor." He looked inside at the pulled-up sheet. "Looks like I'm too late. Your husband?"

"No." Maud stood up. "I'm Mrs. Kackley's sister."

"Sure. I remember. I heard you were taking care of Nelson."

"I was here every minute tonight," she said. "But he just slipped away."

"That means he had an easy time," Doc said. "Sorry

I took so long getting here, but the stationmaster's wife was having boys."

"Twins?"

"Sure thing. Two more citizens for Abilene."

Maud built up the fire, and fried potatoes and bacon for the doctor, after which he sent her to her bed behind the curtain, saying he was used to sitting up. She worried aloud about the burial and Mr. Nelson's sweetheart, but Doc promised they would sort it out in the morning. She went to bed without undressing.

The next thing Maud knew, it was morning. Someone was chopping wood.

She was embarrassed to find that the doctor had built the fire and the kettle was boiling. It was still early, the sun not yet up.

"Who's your nearest neighbor?" the doctor asked.

"The Coddington boys."

Doc made a face. "Well, it couldn't hurt to ask one of them to sit with the body while you're gone. I'll ride back to town with you, and we can stop at Kackley's on the way and ask your sister to lay him out. Maybe Kackley will dig the grave. Was Nelson any kin?"

Maud shook her head.

"I'll meet the train with you," Doc said, "and help you tell his sweetheart. Then you can bring her back with the coffin and bury him tomorrow."

It was such a relief to have someone tell her what to do that Maud didn't even mind wading through dew-wet grass to find Sam, Mr. Nelson's horse. Her skirt was wet to her waist by the time she found the horse, but he took the bridle willingly enough. The wind dried her skirt before she reached the Coddington's dugout.

No smoke was coming from the chimney when she rode down into the creek bed that formed their dooryard. She arrived just as Eph stumbled through the open door, pulling up his suspenders. He ran his fingers through his hair when he saw Maud.

"Ain't you calling kinda early?" he asked, squinting as though the light hurt his eyes.

"Doc sent me," Maud said. "Mr. Nelson died last night."

Jake emerged from the dugout, buttoning his shirt. "Eph, start the fire," he ordered over his shoulder while he looked Maud up and down. "What does Doc want?" he growled.

"He wants to know if you'll sit with Mr. Nelson's body till my sister comes. I'm going to town with him to fetch the coffin."

Jake scowled up at her. "Told you he was a goner."

Maud gritted her teeth. "Will you come?"

"Why not? Nothin' else to do for excitement. I'll be over when I've had my coffee. Where you want him planted?"

Maud hadn't had time to consider that question. She knew Mr. Nelson's land as well as anyone; it was probably for her to decide. The grave ought to be off by itself—one of the corners. Of course a single grave didn't take much space. At the thought of the loneliness, tears started to her eyes, but she forced them back. She mustn't cry in front of the Coddingtons. They were rough; it would be dangerous to show any weakness.

"The northeast corner," she told Jake. The land was high, but not rocky.

Jake hawked and spat. "Couldn't you think of no place further?"

"That's where he'd want to be," Maud said with finality.

"All right, sister. I'll bring a jug and a spade," Jake said. "Eph can fetch Charlie and Shorty." He turned away, his brown hair rumpled, his shirt none too clean.

Maud wished she hadn't asked him. She should have told Doc it would be better to ride further and get Charlie Dexter, but it was too late now. She hoped the other men would keep the Coddingtons from getting rowdy. She kicked bare heels into Sam's flanks and rode off.

Back at Mr. Nelson's soddy, Maud put Sam in the lean-to beside Doc's horse and went in to see what Doc had done about breakfast.

Her eyes opened wide. Breakfast was all ready. Doc had made tea and cornmeal mush. Maud brought out what molasses was left, and they ate in companionable silence.

She was hitching Sam to the wagon when Jake rode in. He followed her inside and thumped his burlap-covered jug on the table.

"Little early for that," Doc said.

"Can't see it's any of your business," Jake snarled.

"No, it's not," Doc agreed. "Ready, Maud?"

Outside Doc set his bag on the wagon seat, threw his saddle into the back, and tied his horse to the tailgate. Maud snatched her shawl and sunbonnet from the peg, and Doc handed her the reins.

She felt very adult as Sam clip-clopped the two

miles across the empty prairie to Kackley's little shanty.

Her sister Iva was working in the garden. The two children and the baby were playing in the dirt.

Iva's huband, George Kackley, was better off than most settlers because he owned two yoke of oxen and a heavy breaking plow. He had a whole list of folks who wanted him to break the sod on their places. But the money he earned all went to the bank to pay for the oxen and their fine stable. Iva was lucky if she could buy a little cloth for the children's dresses. Maud hadn't had a new dress in over a year, and the way she was outgrowing this one was embarrassing. Everything had to wait till George could plow his own acres, wait till the oxen were paid for, wait till George got his first good crop. Meantime, with Maud out of the house, they were spared an extra mouth to feed, though she knew her sister sadly missed her company. With George away working for days at a time, Iva was left alone with the children.

Still, Maud didn't want to go back there. George Kackley was crude. Sometimes when he drank, he knocked Iva around. He said Maud was too fine-nosed, just because she tried to keep the house nice. More than anything in the world Maud wanted a nice home.

"I'll go right over," Iva told the doctor. Maud knew Iva was glad of the break in the day-to-day monotony of the claim. Iva was brown and skinny, and two teeth were missing from her smile.

"You'll stop and tell George where I've gone, won't you?" she asked. "He's plowing over to Miller's. It's right on your way. Is there potatoes?" she asked Maud. "I'll cook something for dinner."

They stopped to tell George, Maud's brother-in-law.

"You'll be coming home then," George said to Maud. "Iva's missed you."

"She'll be needed awhile yet," Doc said.

After they drove away, Doc asked, "Your sister's husband treat you all right?"

Maud felt her face burn. Reluctantly she knew what he meant. But how had he guessed? She supposed he could see with his own eyes that she was growing womanly. Beneath her shawl, her old dress stretched tight across the bosom.

"I might not go back there," she said airily. "Mister Nelson made me promise to try to get his sweetheart to stay on the claim. I promised to stay with her."

"A lady homesteader? Heavens to Betsy!" Doc laughed, then sobered. "Might do. If she's bringing a little cash. Anyway, what I want to say, young lady, is that if Kackley gives you any trouble, you pack up and come to town. I know several ladies who'd be glad to have a hired girl."

Maud's heart leaped. Did he know she was only thirteen? If he thought she was older, so much the better. Not to have to go back to the Kackleys—no matter what! She blushed for her family, and then thought angrily, George Kackley isn't my family. Still, she felt embarrassed for her sister, who'd been fool enough to marry him.

Sam trotted along the dusty track that had worn a dent in the prairie grass. The July sun blazed in the cloudless sky. Mirages shimmered in the distance. But the hot, steady wind fanned the girl, the man, and the horse, drying their sweat and keeping them from discomfort.

"It was better this way," Doc said, referring to Mr. Nelson's death. "There's no cure for consumption. Some doctors believe it's catching."

"I'll miss him," Maud said. "He treated me like I was somebody."

Doc smiled. "That's as good an epitaph as a man could ask."

"What's an epitaph?"

"It's what they carve on gravestones, back East."

Maud's own parents were buried back on the Kentucky farm where she'd been born, the farm George Kackley had sold to get money to move west. He'd been right to move. He'd been a soldier, too, so he could claim for free a whole hundred and sixty acres, without a stone or a tree on it. All a farmer had to do was break up the sod and wait a year for it to rot. As soon as the first crops came in, everyone would be rich.

Meanwhile folks had to tough it out.

· 2 ·
An
Arrival

SOME MILES outside Abilene they forded the Smoky Hill River, dried-up and shallow this time of year. The flat prairie in all directions was brown and dusty.

"What happened to all the grass?" Maud asked in astonishment.

"Trails herds," Doc said. "Like that bunch over there. And there's another." He pointed to faraway patches of brown. "There's more cattle than ever this year. They've eaten up the grass for miles around while they're waiting to be shipped. You'll be surprised how the town has grown. When the rest of the country realizes the brilliant future we have, and the opportunity, and the healthy climate, why Abilene's going to rival St. Louis. There's been talk about moving the national capital here. They ought to. The exact center of the United States is right over at Fort Riley."

Maud was excited. She hadn't been to town since early spring when she'd started working for Mr. Nelson. Charlie Dexter or Shorty Haynes, who lived farther along the track, had done her shopping and brought back Mr. Nelson's mail.

Sure enough, houses had sprung up in every direction. Store buildings were filling in the empty lots along Texas Street.

"I took the measurements for the coffin," Doc said. "Did Nelson leave any money?"

Maud nodded. Mr. Nelson had entrusted her with all his cash—fifty-two dollars. The bills were pinned in the pocket of her dress.

"All right," Doc said, "we'll stop by the coffinmaker's first. Do you have shopping to do?"

"Yes." Maud held the list in her head—coffee, tea, a little sugar to offer the mourners. As for buying other supplies, that depended on what Miss Warren decided. If Miss Warren couldn't be convinced to take over the claim, then Maud would give her what was left of Mr. Nelson's money after paying for the doctor and the coffin.

At the back of Doc's two-room office was a stable. Maud unhitched Sam and made him comfortable. Doc opened his office for business.

At the nearest general store Maud made her purchases. She also spent a nickel on half a yard of black cloth. Back at Doc's she cut and folded a strip to make an armband to show that she was in mourning. Doc pinned it around the sleeve of her dress until it could be sewn properly. Miss Warren might want an armband, too, if she didn't have a black dress. At any rate, the rest of the cloth wouldn't be wasted; Maud could always use it for her quilt.

At noon Doc took her to dinner at the hotel, the most genteel thing Maud had ever done. For a time she forgot her sadness at Mr. Nelson's death and her dread of the coming meeting.

After dinner there was nothing to do but sit in Doc's office, because a girl her age couldn't walk up and down the street unless she had errands; and loafers hung out at the railroad station. She wished she had brought her piece bag. In a whole afternoon she could have put together at least three blocks. Two patients came to consult with the doctor. One man brought a bag of oats in part payment of his bill.

At last it was time to pick up the coffin. Maud put Sam back between the shafts of the wagon, and Doc locked his office.

"If I didn't," he explained, "some of these fools would sneak in and drink the alcohol."

The coffin was plain pine, the outside stained black with stove polish. The coffinmaker slid it into the back of the wagon, Maud paid him, and they drove to the station. When Miss Warren saw the black box and Maud's armband, she would know.

The train was late . . . more waiting . . . but at the depot, at least, something was going on. Doc and four other men argued about Texas fever—the deadly cattle disease that spread wherever longhorns walked. Texans denied its existence. Texas cattle didn't have the sickness, so how could they be spreading it?

The train came clanging in, puffing smoke and steam. The passengers came down the steps—dusty-looking men, a fat woman with a little girl, and then a young lady wearing a soft gray dress and a straw bonnet. Was that Miss Warren? She looked over the crowd as though expecting someone. She was the only young lady to get off. Maud's stomach felt cold with sorrow.

Doc stepped forward, removed his hat, and bowed.

"Miss Warren?"

"Yes—" She was on the platform now, a little bit of a thing, hardly taller than Maud. In one glance she had taken in the crowd and the town. She looked terrified.

"I'm Doctor Owen. This young lady is Maud Kackley."

"McPherson," Maud corrected.

"McPherson," the doctor repeated. "I'm afraid we have sad news for you. Mr. Nelson passed away last night."

Miss Warren's pale face grew perfectly white. Maud thought she was going to faint. Doc took her arm. "We've got Nelson's wagon here," he said soothingly. "We're going to take you to my office first. Here's your carpetbag. You can wash your face there, or cry, or do whatever you want without a lot of fools gaping at you. Maud will make you some tea."

"My trunks," she said faintly.

"I'll come back for them," Doc said. He assisted her onto the wagon seat. Maud took the reins. Doc sat in back on the coffin.

Miss Warren pulled a lace handkerchief from her reticule and dabbed at her eyes.

"I'm sorry," she apologized. "What did you say your name was?"

"Maud McPherson. I've been taking care of Mr. Nelson. He was awful nice."

Tears ran down Miss Warren's cheeks. She held the handkerchief to her trembling mouth.

Maud gave Sam the signal to start.

"Did you say last night?" the young woman whispered.

"Yes."

"Then he hasn't been buried?"

"No." Maud kept her eyes on the horse's ears. "He tried to hold out till you got here."

"I was afraid from his letters that he was getting worse," Miss Warren said. "That's why I insisted on coming. I hoped I could—" Her voice broke, and she could not continue.

At his office Doc made Miss Warren some brandy with her tea. "You'll need to bear up awhile longer," he told her. "Maud's going to take you out to the claim, and she'll stay there with you."

"You're both very kind," she choked out.

Doc said, "If you'd like to lie down, please use my bedroom. Look after her," he told Maud. "I'll go back for the trunks. Don't leave her alone to brood."

Doc returned, bringing a kettle of soup from the hotel. They coaxed Miss Warren to swallow a few spoonfuls. Maud was hungry. She refilled her bowl so she could eat more of the store-bought crackers.

It was close to sundown when Maud and Miss Warren said goodbye to Doc and set off. The sun was setting in a red glow that covered the whole of the western sky above the flat horizon. In the east the sky was pale green. Maud kept thinking of questions to ask, but Miss Warren's grief had to be respected.

The sky darkened. Sam plodded steadily. The moon rose full and bright, casting the moving shadow of the wagon on the tall grass.

Lightning began to flash in the south, lighting up a bank of clouds.

Miss Warren spoke at last. "Is it going to rain?"

Maud liked her voice. It was low-pitched and breathless—as though she was excited about something. And still she spoke like a lady.

"It's heat lightning," Maud explained. "It comes, this time of year."

"Have we far to go?"

"Ten miles."

Miss Warren untied her bonnet and held it in her lap. She pushed back wisps of light brown hair that had escaped the knot atop her head and drew a shaky breath.

"This country is so big," she said softly. "It makes my affairs seem insignificant."

Insignificant. Maud savored the word. It must mean small. She wondered if she should tell Miss Warren about taking over the claim. No, it would be better to wait until Mr. Nelson was buried.

The long drive passed almost in silence. From time to time Maud dozed. Miss Warren sat upright, staring into the darkness.

Once she asked, "Is somebody—with him?" Another time she said, "How can you tell where you're going?"

"We're following a track," Maud explained. "Sam knows the way home."

When they reached the claim, the moonlight showed the shapes of two men sitting in the dooryard. Inside the house the kerosene lamp glowed softly.

Maud recognized her brother-in-law. The other man spoke—it was Charlie Dexter. He came forward to introduce himself to Miss Warren and help her down from the wagon. "This here's George Kackley," Maud heard him say. "I guess you ladies would like some tea. I'll build up a fire." He seemed more talkative than usual. Maud caught a whiff of his breath and knew why. He'd been drinking whisky.

"I guess you'd like to see him," Charlie said to Miss Warren and led her inside. Drawn by the light, the insects swooping around the room were like an invasion. Charlie removed the vinegar-soaked cloth covering Mr. Nelson's face. Miss Warren gazed and turned away sobbing.

Maud went quickly outside to bring in her purchases. Her brother-in-law was unloading the coffin.

"As soon as you ladies turn in," he said with awesome politeness, "we're going to put Nelson in this box and take him down to the creek where it's cooler. Otherwise he won't keep."

Maud's sister had baked cornbread before going home with the children. Miss Warren ate a tiny piece and drank a cup of tea. Then she and Maud retired behind the curtain.

"What a relief to take off these corsets," Miss Warren murmured.

SOON AFTER DAYLIGHT everyone assembled for the burial. Shorty Haynes came in his wagon with his children, Bud and Luanne. He brought a covered pan from the wagon and set it on the table. Taking off the covering cloth, he stepped back proudly. The pan held three roasted prairie chickens. Maud thanked him, and when Miss Warren came from behind the curtain neatly dressed and combed and wearing a black dress, Maud was careful to introduce her.

Next Iva walked in, carrying the baby and a pan of gingerbread. Her other two youngsters tagged behind.

The Coddingtons rode up, with yet another jug. The men stood around outside, drinking whisky for breakfast. Inside Maud, Iva, and Miss Warren drank coffee and made awkward conversation.

At last Charlie Dexter came to the door. "I reckon we're ready to start," he said. "Bring Nelson's Bible," he told Maud. "Shorty's going to read."

The men raised the coffin to their shoulders and set out. The women and children followed, Maud carrying the baby. The sun was already blazing as they filed down to the hollow where the springs made a wide, shallow pool. Upstream from the pool the creek was dry. Its opposite bank was a limestone cliff, higher than Abilene's tallest building.

The procession wound up the dry limestone bed of the creek to a gully that led to the high ground.

"My, why are they taking him so far?" Iva asked.

"I chose the spot," Maud said. "I thought that's where he'd want to be." Iva said no more, and Maud was impressed with herself. Even Jake Coddington had gone along with her choice.

Up on the level they crossed through knee-deep grass to the raw hole. Maud shifted the baby to her other hip and looked about, approving her decision. Grass was sparser here, and pink prairie roses fluttered in the wind. The ground was high; one could see miles in every direction.

The coffin was lowered by means of two ropes already in place. Shorty Haynes read from Psalms, and Charlie Dexter raised his voice in "Shall We Gather at the River." The rest joined in as best they could. Then Iva led Miss Warren away. Maud followed, still with the baby, who had been good and quiet. The men sent the other children away, too, except Bud, who was old enough to stay while they filled the grave.

By the time the three women reached the house, Miss Warren's face had turned a sickly white.

"It's the heat!" Iva exclaimed. She steered Miss Warren to Mr. Nelson's one proper chair. Miss Warren untied her bonnet strings, and Iva removed it for her. Iva held it a moment like something precious before she handed it to Maud to put on the bed behind the curtain.

Mr. Nelson's bed, where he had spent so much time of late, had been plumped up and covered with a comforter.

"Put baby on the bed and find something to fan Miss Warren with," Iva directed. "Drink this," she told Miss Warren, "and try to eat something." She poured a cup of cold tea and stirred sugar into it.

"I'll be all right in a minute," Miss Warren protested. "It's—it's everything at once."

"Of course."

Maud found an old newspaper to use for a fan. Iva carved the prairie chickens, cut gingerbread and cornbread, and made more coffee.

Maud put out the sugar. Luanne, who was six, was given the job of shooing flies off the food with a dishtowel. Maud felt that Mr. Nelson would be pleased if he could see how well it was all managed. The two Kackley children were quietly happy at having a new yard to play in, with different dirt.

The heat increased. The men returned. They chose pieces of prairie chicken and cornbread and took them outside, where they stood talking and eating. Everyone had to take turns drinking coffee, for there were only three cups.

The sun beat down on the sod-roofed room until it was stifling. Maud envied the men outside. Miss Warren looked limp.

"She's pale as a ghost," Iva whispered. "Get her to lie down as soon as everyone leaves."

If only they would! The trouble was, they were all glad of a chance to talk to their neighbors.

At last George Kackley put his head in the door. Whisky always turned his face red. He looked more repulsive than ever.

"Come on," he said.

Iva picked up the baby. "I'm real glad to have met you, Miss Warren. I'm sorry it had to be on such a sad occasion."

Maud took momentary pride in her sister. She

might be scrawny and work-worn, but she'd learned real good manners from Ma and Pa, and she hadn't forgotten them.

"You can bring the gingerbread pan when you come home," she was saying to Maud.

Miss Warren walked with Iva to the doorstep, where George waited. George raised his hat. "Nelson was a good man. We'll miss him. I'd appreciate it if you'd give me first chance to buy his horse, Miss Warren. We done quite a lot for him, one way and another, lending him Little Sister here."

Before Maud could protest her brother-in-law's words, Miss Warren put her hand to her forehead. "I don't know—" she began, and fainted. George caught her, staggering with the unexpectedness of it.

They laid her on Mr. Nelson's bed. Iva dabbed her brow with a damp rag sprinkled with vinegar. Miss Warren soon came round and was coaxed to sit in the rocker.

The men filed in quietly, hats in hand, to take their leave. Iva and George left, the children tagging behind. A few minutes later Maud and Miss Warren were alone. George had not repeated his request to buy the horse.

"At last I can take off my corsets," Miss Warren said faintly. "Is it always this hot?"

"It's hot in summer," Maud acknowledged. "But we don't spend much time inside. It's better outside in the shade, where there's a wind."

"Should we move out there?"

"Would you rather lie down?" Maud asked.

"Maybe I will," Miss Warren said.

Maud brought out the three pieces of prairie

chicken she had put aside and ate one of them with cornbread. She drank a cup of coffee with sugar. Miss Warren slept and slept. Maud covered the food with the dishtowel and decided to go look at the grave. Later, if she could come by some nice wood, she would make a cross for it. Meantime . . . She put the spade over her shoulder and picked up the water bucket.

On the way she looked for Sam. He wasn't inclined to wander, but it was best to keep an eye on one's animals. In the same way she counted the five chickens every night before she shut them into their sod house.

Sam was in the cottonwood grove at the downstream end of the spring-fed pool. Beyond the hollow and the grove, the land rose to the level of the prairie. The overflow from the pool trickled along a smooth limestone bed between high banks.

The grave looked as Maud expected, the clods mounded high. She dug up a clump of prairie roses and replanted it at the foot, then carried water all the way up from the pool, made a little trench around the roots, and filled it with water.

When she got back to the house, Miss Warren was still asleep.

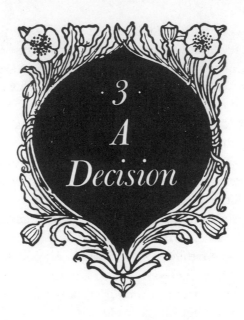

·3·
A
Decision

MISS WARREN did not wake until almost sunset. Maud had carried the rocker outdoors to the shady side of the house. She suggested that Miss Warren come outside.

Miss Warren hesitated. "Oh, dear, I should put on my corsets. But it's so warm!"

"Iva don't never wear hers anymore."

"*Doesn't* wear, or never wears."

"Never wears," Maud repeated. She must watch her tongue, and remember Miss Warren had been a schoolteacher.

Miss Warren dropped into the rocker with a sigh. Maud brought a keg from the house to sit on.

"This is pleasant," Miss Warren said after a bit. "I wonder—is there any food left?"

Maud sprang up. "I saved you two pieces of chicken. Do you want some gingerbread?"

The rest of the prairie chicken had been eaten. Maud satisfied her hunger with gingerbread. The sun sank, the long prairie evening began. Maud and Miss Warren sat in quiet harmony, speaking now and again about the events of the day.

Then Maud spied two horsemen coming from the east. One horse had a white stocking.

"The Coddingtons!" she exclaimed. Despite the heat, she felt a warning shiver. "What in thunder do they want?"

Miss Warren sat up. "My dear, your language! Oh, I *knew* I shouldn't come out without my corsets. I can't run into the house now! They've seen us out here."

"If you just sit there, they won't notice."

"But ladies get up to welcome guests!"

"Jake and Eph won't know that," Maud said scornfully.

The men rode their horses to the watering trough and dismounted. Leaving the horses to drink, they approached the house. Fortunately, they didn't seem drunk. Maud and Miss Warren remained glued to their seats.

"Good evening, ladies." Jake sounded as soft as molasses. Maud relaxed slightly.

"Good evening," Maud and Miss Warren chorused.

Jake kicked Eph's foot. Eph mumbled, "Good evening."

"I reckoned it wouldn't be too early to talk about Nelson's claim," Jake began. "I don't want some other fellow getting the jump on us. Eph's turned twenty-one. When we heard Nelson was a goner, we figured Eph could take over—buy up the relinquishment."

"I don't know how that's done," Miss Warren whispered.

"I know it's early," Jake contradicted himself. "But Eph's been nagging me."

Maud had much ado not to snort at the idea of poor Eph daring to nag his brother.

Jake rolled up the chopping block and sat on it. Eph squatted on his heels and chewed on a grass blade. Both men were downwind. They smelled strongly of horses and sweaty clothing. Maud hoped it wouldn't give Miss Warren a distaste for everything. She began to feel really frightened. What if Miss Warren said yes to Jake before Maud had a chance to tell her what Mr. Nelson had said?

She spoke first, though it wasn't polite. "There's good land further south!" She turned to Miss Warren as though explaining the country. "A person can get a hundred-and-sixty acres there if they want, instead of eighty, because it's so far from the railroad."

Jake shook his head. "We want claims side by side so we can put up a soddy." He gave Maud a warning glare, and then glanced at Miss Warren from under his brows. "I'd be willing to offer a hundred dollars. Eph's not obliged to offer anything, you know. Can't nobody inherit because Nelson wasn't married."

Eph added, "We could make a lot of trouble for anybody else." In the fading light his dull eyes took on a mean squint.

"Wouldn't advise anybody to try." Jake laughed.

Maud's stomach cramped with fear. At the same time, she grew angry. "You got no right talking like that, the very evening of the burial!"

"Yeah?" Eph sneered. "Your brother-in-law already bid for the horse. I suppose that's all right!"

"Shut up, Eph. We ain't here about the horse." Jake took his knife from its scabbard and absently sharpened it against his boot.

Miss Warren put her hand to her brow. "I need time to think," she said faintly.

"Overnight, maybe? We'll stop by tomorrow morning." Jake got to his feet. "Come on, Eph."

"Maud, dear, is there any tea left?" Miss Warren asked as the brothers mounted.

Maud poured the last of the tea into Miss Warren's cup. She sipped it slowly until a dip in the land hid the riders. Then she looked at Maud with steady eyes. "I wonder what Mr. Nelson would have wanted me to do?"

Maud could have shouted with relief. "He made me promise to talk to you!" she cried. "But I didn't like to do it before—before he was buried. He—" The idea didn't sound so wonderful now that she'd seen Miss Warren, who was so dainty and frail-looking, like lace.

But Miss Warren's eyes had brightened. "Did he leave me a message? I'm so glad! I didn't ask, for fear you'd say he was too sick."

"He did!" Maud exclaimed. "He wanted me to tell you to stay here."

"*Stay* here! But how could I?" Miss Warren demanded. "I'm not his widow."

"You could claim the land for yourself!" Maud cried. "Mr. Nelson said you could. He said, if she moves fast, she can take over my claim. She'll be better off here than with her brother." Maud didn't think Mr. Nelson meant her to repeat the part about withering. " 'Tell her,' he said 'it's the best quarter section around.' He said he wished you'd try it for a year."

A tear rolled down Miss Warren's cheek. "I can't tell you how good it is to know he was thinking of me. We both knew he might not live many years, but I'd hoped—" Her voice became suspended.

Above the garden lightning bugs began to dance. Maud stiffened. A black, furry animal was waddling among the bean rows. That danged skunk! This was no time to race out there and chase it away. Maud picked up a piece of kindling and flung it among the pumpkin vines. Perhaps the noise would scare it off.

"Why did you do that?" Miss Warren was wiping her eyes.

"Skunk."

The animal slipped away. It would come back in the night, no doubt, but it didn't need to get the idea it could drop in for a feed when folks were sitting right in the yard.

"Mr. Nelson really wanted me to stay here? Alone?" Miss Warren's eyes swept the circle of gathering night.

"Not alone," Maud said shyly. "He made me promise to stay with you. If you want me. The land's free, and it's the best in the United States. Everyone says so."

"Hmmm." Miss Warren looked thoughtful.

"It won't always be like this," Maud hastened to explain. "People are moving in all the time. Abilene's growing so fast! All the railroad company's sections are sold to investors. Before you know it, we'll have lots of neighbors."

"Your sister seems to be the only woman neighbor now. Isn't there a Mrs. Haynes?"

"Mrs.—? Oh, you mean Bud and Luanne's mother! No, I think she died. There's Mrs. Martin. The Martins live over there."

Miss Warren glanced over her shoulder. Since the sod house was encircled by waving grasses planted either by Nature or man, the view was the same in every direction. Now, with night coming on, the land stretched velvet and mysterious from horizon to horizon. The sky was still gray, but a few stars were already shining.

"I find it hard to believe we're not alone on the earth," Miss Warren said. "How do people stand it?"

Maud bit her lip. "Mostly they have to. Once they've got a house built, it aint—*isn't*—safe to go away and leave it. Claim jumpers might move in. The Coddingtons aren't very far away. Quarter of a mile, I guess. Not that a person would choose them for neighbors. Though they did tell the doctor to come when I asked them. But it's only another quarter-mile beyond them to Shorty Haynes's place, and Charlie Dexter is just beyond him."

"I see." Miss Warren's voice did not betray what she was thinking.

"The Martins are black folks from down South," Maud explained.

Miss Warren's eyes widened. "Freed slaves?"

Maud considered. "They might be. They have five children, younger than me—Eulalia, Horace, Cora, Sammy, and Eliza. Eliza starts school next year."

"What did that disgusting man mean about putting up a sod house together?"

"Jake? Oh, they'd build a house across the boundary line, half on Jake's land, half on Eph's. They'd live together and still be living on their own claims, like the law makes you do. Jake's been too lazy to build a soddy, so far. They live like coyotes in a cave in the creek bank."

"If I can't inherit the claim, why did he offer me a hundred dollars?"

"For the relinquishment, I guess." It was a word Maud had heard a lot, but she wasn't sure what it was. "I think if you go to the land office first, you'd have first choice to take out a new claim on this place, but if you don't want to, you relinquish it to someone else."

"That makes sense. The other party would give me a hundred dollars to step out of the picture."

Maud nodded. "It's a valuable claim. On account of the springs and the pool. Mr. Randolph, north of here, would love to get hold of the pool for his cattle. That might be why Jake and Eph are in such a hurry."

Miss Warren began to ask a great many questions: what crops had been planted, and what work had been done, what work still had to be done. It was easy to see she'd lived on a farm. She asked how Maud had managed to do all the chores and look after a sick man, too.

Maud explained how there wasn't much work to do. Holding down a claim wasn't really farming. First the thick carpet of grass roots that covered the prairie had to be plowed. When Mr. Nelson first came, he had paid George Kackley to cut sod to build the house and plow the ten acres the government said had to be planted. Most of the neighbors were in the same boat, trying to scrape by on garden truck and hunting until they could somehow get all their land plowed and raise crops. Few of them had livestock. Pigs and cows were hard to get, even if one had money. Stock had to come from the East.

"The only thing that has to be done" Maud finished, "is water the chickens and gather the eggs. And check on Sam sometimes."

"But how will the people who don't own plows and oxen ever get all their land plowed?" Miss Warren asked.

Maud puzzled over the question. "I guess they're just hoping," she said finally. "Nobody wants to go back to their kinfolks broke. If they can hang on five years, the land's theirs. Then I guess they can borrow some money . . ."

"What about winter?" Miss Warren asked.

"There's ten acres of sod corn. Mr. Nelson thought that would yield enough cornmeal to last. Sam eats prairie hay. There's plenty of that, as you can see. I could cut some every day with a sickle. We could bring it to the house in the wagon and build a haystack. That's not hard work."

"Won't your sister want you back?"

Maud wrinkled her nose. "Her husband looks at me funny."

"Oh." Miss Warren understood what she meant.

"I have a little money," Miss Warren said thoughtfully. "My brother bought out my share of our parents' farm. He and Silas—Mr. Nelson—never got along. Silas came from a poor, stony farm in the hills. My brother never had any use for anyone poorer than himself. Including me, though I paid my way."

"What did you do?"

"Taught school."

"You could do that here!" Maud bounced excitedly. "The teacher last year left."

Miss Warren's eyes brightened once more. "Maybe I could! Silas was right. Almost anything would be better than going back to my brother's." Her eyes lost their shine. "But do we dare? Jake Coddington seems determined to take over."

"I don't *think* he'd harm two females," Maud said. "He'll be mad, though," she added honestly.

"The whole frontier is dangerous," Miss Warren mused. "Back East we hear it's full of outlaws."

"The Coddingtons are the only ones I know of," Maud said. And they haven't really done anything. Abilene might be dangerous when the Texans are there. But I've never seen anyone get shot."

"You sound sorry!" Miss Warren smiled. "I suppose Mr. Nelson must have thought I'd be safe."

"Then you'll stay?" Maud's voice squeaked.

"He said he wanted me to stay a year?" Miss Warren asked sadly.

"Yes."

"I suppose I could. We wouldn't be burning any bridges. You could always go back to your sister. I can always go back to my brother and be an old maid schoolteacher."

"And you'll be doing what Mr. Nelson wanted," Maud urged.

"So what have we to lose?" Miss Warren sounded

almost light-hearted. "If you think the Coddingtons won't shoot us—?"

Maud looked horrified. "They wouldn't dare do that! The neighbors would hang them."

"That wouldn't do us much good," Miss Warren said. She took a deep breath. "All right, what do I have to do to defy the Coddingtons?"

· 4 ·
Filing
a Claim

"YOU'RE SURE you know the way?" Miss Warren repeated.

"Oh, yes! If we take the road east, there's no way
we can get lost."

Again Maud and Miss Warren were seated in the
wagon behind Sam. This time the sun was barely over
the rim of the prairie. They had risen and breakfasted
in the dark. As soon as she could see, Maud had slipped
through the wet grass to the creek, caught Sam and
harnessed him to the wagon. Then they had set out for
the land office at Junction City.

Miss Warren was wearing her black dress and black
bonnet. Maud had sewed her armband neatly to her
sleeve.

"What if the Coddingtons overtake us?" Miss Warren asked.

"We'll lose out." Maud tried to glance over her shoulder, but she was wearing one of the new sunbonnets Miss Warren had brought. The bonnet's brim limited her vision to straight ahead.

"There's no chance they'll *overtake* us," Maud said carefully, "because we're going by way of Abilene and take the road. The Coddingtons will ride crosscountry. That's faster and they could get there before us. But they're lazy. They're probably not even up yet. By the time they catch their horses and ride over to talk to you, the morning will be half-gone."

"I hope you're right. Now that I've decided to go through with this, I'd be disappointed if they beat us to it."

Maud and Miss Warren had laid their plans the night before. Maud knew what had to be done. At the land office Miss Warren must explain why Mr. Nelson's claim to the land was cancelled and that she wished to file her own claim and start over.

This time of year the road between Abilene and Junction City was one continuous cloud of dust from the wheels of freight wagons and west-bound settlers. At noon Maud stopped in a cottonwood grove along the river. A family group nearby had built a noonday fire. They begged Miss Warren and Maud to accept cups of coffee to drink with their cornbread.

The afternoon was ending by the time they drove down the main street of Junction City. They were tired and hot and incredibly dusty. On one of the buildings a sign read:

U.S. LAND OFFICE
BARGAINS IN LAND

But the door was shut and locked. Miss Warren rented a room at the hotel.

With pleasure they stripped off their dusty dresses and washed their faces and arms in the big china wash-bowl the room provided. Maud longed to see the town, which was bigger and older than Abilene, but she curbed her impatience. Miss Warren mustn't faint again, and she wasn't used to such hot weather. So Maud agreed to share the double bed for an hour's rest before going down to the dining room for supper.

After supper Miss Warren asked the hotel clerk what time the land office opened. He advised her to get there early; a crowd would collect long before it opened. No, nothing special. There was always a crowd.

They walked out then to see the town, but the number of men lounging along the board sidewalk soon made them feel out of place. They walked briskly back to the hotel. Maud was disappointed.

"We'll look around tomorrow," Miss Warren promised. "This is the first time I've ever had money without my father or my brother to tell me how to spend it," she confided. "I'm going to spend some of it on nice things."

"What?"

"You'll see." A glimmer appeared for a moment in Miss Warren's eyes, making Maud hope that once the sadness of Mr. Nelson's death was past, the two of them might find a great many things to enjoy together.

"I FEEL AS THOUGH I'm never going to stop being tired," Miss Warren said as they fell into bed. "I believe I could sleep twenty-four hours, but I asked the clerk to call us early."

Despite the hot room Maud fell asleep almost before she could appreciate the wonderfully comfortable bed.

Minutes later—it seemed—she was awakened by the sound of pistol shots. Miss Warren was crouched on the edge of the bed in her nightgown. The almost-bare room was bright with moonlight.

"What's going on?" Maud muttered.

"I don't know!"

The noise had awakened every dog in town. The room's one window overlooked the street, and the disturbance seemed to be across the street. Maud bounded out of bed. Before she reached the window a raucous "Yippee!" followed by a flurry of hoofbeats sent the town dogs into a frenzy of barking.

"Stay back!" Miss Warren cried, but the hoofbeats were already growing fainter in the dust. Maud leaned out in time to see the flash as one of three riders fired his pistol skyward.

She returned to bed. "Those were cowboys. Shorty Haynes told me how they celebrate. They drive cattle up from Texas. It takes weeks. When they get the cows here to the railroad, they get paid and they take a holiday."

Miss Warren shuddered. "I'm glad Mr. Nelson

didn't ask me to live in town. My nerves couldn't have stood it."

Maud was not surprised. All ladies had "nerves." For herself, she found the noise and excitement exhilarating. She was glad she wasn't old enough yet to have nerves. She was old enough to wear corsets, but George Kackley wouldn't waste money on his wife's sister. For that Maud was grateful.

She tried to stay awake in case something more happened, but the faint jangle of a piano somewhere lulled her. When she next woke, the sky was growing light. Miss Warren was urging her to get up. Somewhere a rooster was crowing.

After a hurried breakfast, they sallied forth. The night's heavy dew had settled the dust of the street, but a passing wagon had already made the day's first wheel tracks in it. Four men were waiting before the land office when Miss Warren and Maud arrived. The men lifted their hats and said good morning, then continued talking among themselves.

"I wonder how long we'll have to wait," Miss Warren said in a low voice. A man with a curly brown beard overheard. "Not long, ma'am. I'm told the agents here work pretty hard."

At that moment a clerk in a white shirt came briskly up and unlocked the door's padlock. Men converged from all directions, but with one accord those in front allowed Miss Warren to enter first.

Maud and Miss Warren found themselves in a small space divided by a railing from the rest of the room, which had two desks and shelves piled with ledgers. Each desk was topped by a battered green blotter blotched with ink. The clerk settled himself at a desk and took out pens and paper.

"You don't need to stay," Miss Warren whispered to Maud. "I'll be all right. Go wait for me at the nearest store." She took a coin from her purse. "Buy something you want."

"Take it," she urged when Maud would have refused. "This is a special day. I want you to remember it. We're about to try our independence."

Maud had never before in her life had money to spend for a treat. She almost ran to the nearest store, and then couldn't decided what to buy—candy, ribbons, writing paper—so many things offered themselves.

In the end she bought a blue ribbon that the storekeeper's wife vowed was the color of her eyes. Its weave made it look like moving water.

Her purchase paid for, she went outside to wait. The store's porch had a roof over it and unopened kegs put out to sit on. Maud sat on one. She could see the whole of the main street in either direction; watching the people going about their business was vastly enjoyable. Living in town must be wonderful.

Miss Warren soon arrived. Maud watched her come along the walk. Men's heads turned, hats were doffed. A well-dressed and pretty young lady—the kind you could introduce to your sister—was something they didn't see every day . . . or even every week.

She came up to Maud, her face alight with satisfaction. "I did it!" she exulted. "The whole hundred and sixty acres. The government man told me I could only file a homestead claim on eighty acres because I hadn't been a soldier. Then he said I could buy Silas's other eighty for a dollar and a quarter an acre—a hundred dollars. So I did! The men there all assured me I can sell it again at that price, if our venture doesn't work. Look, here are the papers!" The folded ends peeped out of her drawstring bag.

"Now, let's see what I have on my list—Did you spend your money?"

Shyly Maud showed her the ribbon. Miss Warren approved the choice.

As they went inside the store again, Miss Warren said, "I have curtains ready in one of my trunks. I think we should have a rag carpet. Don't you?"

Maud was too stunned to reply. No one she knew had a carpet.

"It won't seem quite so much like a dirt floor," Miss Warren went on. She asked the storekeeper if someone in town made carpets. Then she bought glass chimneys for the lamp, which would come into steady use as the days grew shorter. She bought two new plates and cups (Mr. Nelson's were sadly cracked and chipped) and a big white pitcher decorated with roses.

"We won't have milk to put in it, but it will give us something pretty to look at," she said defiantly, as though her brother or father were frowning at her.

"We can use it for flowers," Maud enthused, recovering from shock over the carpet. "I know where to get blue wildflowers that look beautiful."

Miss Warren also bought practical things—enough cornmeal and flour to last till Mr. Nelson's corn was harvested and molasses and beans.

They followed the storekeeper's directions to the home of the woman who made carpets. She wove the strips in six-foot lengths. By sewing three strips together, they could have a square rug to fit between Mr. Nelson's bed (as Maud still thought of it) and the curtain, between the door on the south and the cookstove against the north wall.

"But when muddy water drips down from the roof, it'll be ruined," Maud objected.

"Oh—" Miss Warren was taken aback.

"A rug will soak up the water," the rugmaker put in quickly, "and keep you from walking around in the mud. Or you could roll it up."

Maud looked at the woman's smooth, clean floors and wondered if she had ever lived in a house with a dirt floor.

Miss Warren hesitated only a moment. "I think we ought to have it," she told Maud. "We'll get the roof fixed. I'm surprised. It wasn't like Mr. Nelson to have a leaky roof."

Walking back to the hotel, Maud explained that Mr. Nelson's roof, like the rest of the house, was made of sod. The sods were supported by rough boards laid side by side across the top of the walls. It only leaked after prolonged rain, which didn't happen often on the plains.

They had almost reached the hotel when Miss Warren said in a hollow voice, "Unless I'm mistaken, here come the Coddingtons."

"It is! Let's go in here!" But the store they were passing was a barber shop.

Miss Warren clutched Maud's arm. "We might as well get it over with. They have to know sometime."

Jake Coddington recognized them and strode forward, leaving Eph slouching behind.

"What are you folks doing here?" he demanded. From the smell of him, he'd been drinking. He looked red and furious.

"I beg your pardon?" Miss Warren pretended to gasp.

"You heard me! We came to your place to talk business yesterday, and you'd run out. Now we find you here. What are you fixing to pull?"

"Mr. Coddington, I decided to file on the land myself."

"Eph—" Jake roared over his shoulder. "Get over there in that line like I told you!" By now the line from the land office extended along the sidewalk.

Miss Warren said staunchly, "I must tell you, I already have the papers."

"If that ain't like a woman! Sneaking behind our backs. Gimme them papers!" Jake lunged forward.

Crisp steps sounded on the boards behind Maud. The next thing she knew, a stranger wearing stiff new jeans and a new blue shirt had thrust himself under Jake's nose. Almost before Miss Warren and Maud could step out of the way, the stranger's fist caught Jake on the jaw. Next thing Jake was sitting in the dusty street. His hat had landed beside him.

"That's no way to talk to ladies, mister," the man said. He turned to Eph, standing open-mouthed. Across the street men dropped out of the land-office line and came running.

"What was that for?" Eph exclaimed, raising his fists.

"You want a lesson, too, do you?" With another well-aimed blow, the stranger dropped Eph beside his brother. He then lifted his hat and stepped off the sidewalk so that Miss Warren and Maud could pass. "Good day, ladies. I hope these varmits haven't overset you." He spoke with a peculiar drawl.

"Not at all. Thank you, sir." Clasping Maud's arm, Miss Warren hurried her on toward the hotel. Her face was pink with embarrassment, but she looked very pretty.

Maud couldn't keep from exulting. She would have looked back, but Miss Warren pulled her along.

"I hope he hasn't made them our enemies," Miss Warren worried.

"They would have been anyway," Maud said, "as soon as they found out."

"But you said they wouldn't do anything!"

"I didn't think they would." Maud spoke in a small voice. At the time she had been amazed that Miss Warren trusted her judgment.

Now, however, Miss Warren said, "Oh, I shouldn't have listened to a child! They'll probably shoot us in our beds!"

"Mr. Nelson thought you ought to stay," Maud reminded her.

"Did he know Eph Coddington wanted the place? Oh, Maud, what have I gotten us into?"

"I'm glad!" Maud stoutly maintained. "Jake Coddington's a bag of wind. And a bully."

"I hope you're right—that that's all he is."

Presently she spoke again. "Now all we need is for your brother-in-law to get angry when he learns you

want to stay with me, and I'll have the whole country-
side against me."

"No, you won't," Maud promised. "I wouldn't go
back to my sister's anyway. If need be, Doc said he'd
find me work in town."

"I see. Well, we'd better stop and tell your sister
on the way back." Miss Warren squared her small
shoulders. "Get it all over at once, don't you think?"

"Yes, I do." Maud made her voice cheerful. George
Kackley couldn't say much. Her sister Iva was no dunce.

But the visit to town had been spoiled. Miss Warren paid the bill at the hotel and the livery barn, and a
hostler harnessed Sam. They picked up the carpet and
their purchases from the store. In silence they drove out
of town.

Maud would have liked to drive back across country, but she was afraid Miss Warren wouldn't trust her
to find the way, so they went back the way they had
come. They jogged along silently.

Maud went over in her mind all the things the
Coddingtons could do. None of them amounted to anything. If they went so far as to try to kill Miss Warren,
the neighbors would deal with them quickly and finally.
They wouldn't try that.

"People lose out on claims all the time," Maud
said at last. "The loser finds another piece of land he
likes and tries again." A giggle escaped her at the
memory of Jake and Eph sprawled side by side in the
dust.

"What are you laughing at?" Miss Warren asked.

"The Coddingtons. Oh, Miss Warren, I was scared
when that man hit Jake. Weren't you?"

"I was. It was very gentlemanly of him to come to our rescue. Brave, too. Who do you suppose he was?"

"Maybe one of those Texas cowboys," Maud suggested. "They wear hats like that. His boots were different, too. Did you notice?"

"Yes." Miss Warren permitted herself a giggle, and the next thing they were both laughing. They had succeeded in filing the claim. Now they had only to brave it out. The Coddingtons were but one threat in their risky venture.

"We're in this together," Miss Warren said. "I'd like it if you'd call me Belle."

· 5 ·
Settling
In

"EXACTLY HOW MUCH of all this prairie is ours?" Belle
asked the question at breakfast next morning.

They had reached the claim late the night before,
almost too tired to eat, certainly too tired to build a
cooking fire. Maud had unhitched, and Belle had laid
out a supper of cornbread, apples, and well water. They
had shared Maud's bed. "I'll renew the other one tomorrow," Belle murmured before sleep claimed them.

"Ours?" Maud echoed, now.

Belle smiled across her coffee cup. "You're too
young to be half-owner legally, but I think we should
call it *ours*. I wouldn't have stayed here without you.
And since your dear brother-in-law said last night he
never wanted to see you again, you can't call that home."

Maud looked rueful. "He *was* mad, wasn't he?
You were brave to stand up to him.

Belle nodded, eyes wide. "You've no idea how my knees were shaking. At this rate, if I last a year out here, I'll be able to stand up to anything."

"I think we're over the worst," Maud declared. Then to change the subject, "We could hunt for the boundary markers after breakfast."

"Let's do!" Belle sounded enthusiastic. Maud realized she had not yet seen Belle's real self, only a young woman exhausted from a long train ride and then shocked by grief.

While they waited for the dew to dry, they took Mr. Nelson's bed apart, emptied the old hay out of the tick and washed everything. It seemed right; they were making a new start.

When they set out, Belle looked at Maud's bare feet. "Aren't you afraid of snakes?"

"Snakes hear you coming and scoot into the grass," Maud assured her. In her turn she looked at Belle's high-buttoned boots. "If you want to take your shoes off to save them, nobody'll think anything of it. Everyone goes barefoot in summer."

Belle looked amused. "Maybe I will! When we get back."

They started east along the wagon-wheel path. The long grass dragged at their skirts, but Belle was a country girl as well as a schoolteacher.

They found the small pile of stones that marked the beginning of Jake Coddington's eighty acres, and turned east.

Government surveyors had divided the whole of Kansas into sections one mile square. Each boundary line of Belle's quarter of a section was half a mile long.

At the creek bed they turned north. "There's a few more acres on the other side where we buried Mr. Nelson," Maud said, but they didn't go there.

They stayed on the near side of the marshy pool where the springs were, keeping to high, dry land.

"I've seen antelope here a few times," Maud announced. "In the springtime, some mornings the water was covered with ducks and geese on their way north. I hope we'll see some this fall."

"I'm surprised Silas didn't choose a more level piece," Belle mused.

"Oh, no!" Maud was shocked. "These are the only springs on the creek for miles—just about the only place south of the river. If the creek dries up, Mr. Randolph will pay you to water his cattle here."

They found Sam standing among the trees where the pool became a creek again. Walking was easier in the fringe of timber. They followed the curve of the creek till they came to another small pile of stones.

"Martins' land begins there." Maud pointed. "Their house is 'way at the other end. That side of the creek belongs to Mr. Randolph. He raises cattle and horses. He owns more land than anybody around here. He's on the school board, even though he doesn't have any children. The sections around him belong to the railroad. He runs cattle there, too." Maud turned westward. "Here's the corn."

"Silas planted that field, sick as he was?"

Maud shook her head. "He tried to, but he was too weak. Charlie Dexter planted most of it."

"I wish I'd known," Belle said, "so I could have thanked him."

"Charlie'll be coming around," Maud said dryly. "Anyhow, I baked bread for him all spring."

"That was certainly a repayment! Do you know, I've never baked bread. My sister-in-law didn't want me in her kitchen, and of course I was teaching school. Summers I helped with the garden and the sewing, but never with the cooking."

"I can't sew," Maud said wistfully.

"I'll teach you," Belle promised. "You can teach me to cook."

Two-thirds of the field was waist high. The last third was shorter.

"Why is that?" Belle asked.

"It was planted later," Maud explained. "I planted it. Charlie was busy on his own place."

"I'm impressed!" Belle said.

Maud shrugged. "Anybody can do it. Once the sod is plowed, all a person has to do is chop holes in it with an axe and drop in some grains and step on the hole. It's coming along pretty good," she added, eyeing the dusty green stalks.

Not far from the southwest corner of the claim stood the schoolhouse. It was sod, too, about the size of Mr. Nelson's house, with grass growing thick around it. Off behind stood a roofless sod privy.

Belle seemed stricken dumb. Maud ventured to say, "We'll be closer than anybody."

"So we will," Belle agreed, which might have meant anything.

From the schoolhouse they walked back to the house. Already the day had become unbearably hot.

They stopped at the well to haul up a bucketful of cool water.

"Mr. Nelson dug this well before he got so sick," Maud said. While she drank from the tin cup, she watched Belle studying the house. What was Belle thinking?

The house had a door and two windows built into the south wall. The other three walls were without openings. It was a simple shelter, cool in summer and warm in winter. The only tool needed to build it, once the sod had been plowed, was a spade to cut the sod into blocks.

A row of castor beans nearly seven feet tall marked Maud's garden.

"They're not good for much but shade," Maud explained. "But it's nice to see something tall. Mr. Nelson never got a chance to plant trees . . ." Her voice trailed off. Maybe she shouldn't keep bringing up his name.

"Come spring, we'll plant some ourselves," Belle said briskly. "I brought flower seeds, too."

Squash and pumpkin vines spread with lavish abandon over the sun-baked earth. Weeds were springing up between the rows of potatoes and turnips. The onions looked ready to harvest, and the beans needed picking. Maud ran to the house to get a pan, and Belle helped her pick them.

Belle decided that before they put down the new rug, the whole room should be given a thorough cleaning. She had heard that sod houses attracted bedbugs and fleas. It was true, Maud admitted. So even though the day was already becoming a scorcher, they put the table and the rocker, the sitting kegs and the flour barrel outdoors, swept out all the corners and under the beds, and chased the spiders from the boards that held up the sod roof.

"How bad is it when it rains?" Belle asked.

"Water trickles through only if it rains for a couple of days," Maud assured here. "Which isn't often."

"Dirt must sift down, too." Belle continued to eye the ceiling.

Maud nodded. "But men don't bother about that sort of thing. Martins have a sheet fastened to the ceiling over the table."

"What about the rest of the room?"

Maud shrugged. "The dust just falls."

"If we had newspapers, we could paper the ceiling. It's easy to cook flour and water into paste."

The trouble with that idea was that anyone who subscribed to a newspaper was expected to pass it around for the neighbors to read, too. By the time everyone had read it, the paper would be in tatters.

"If my brother sends me our hometown paper, as he promised," Belle said, "we'll just quietly save them till we get enough."

By the time they had laid the rug and put the house back together and filled both bed ticks with new hay, the day was nearly over. They were both tired, but the room looked bright and clean.

"Oh, dear," Belle said, "I did want to get the curtains hung. When Silas wrote that he had two windows, I made curtains, but they still have to be hemmed."

She opened one of her trunks. On top were two quilts. Maud admired them as they were laid aside.

"I started that one when I was twelve," Belle mused.

"That's how old I was when I started mine!" Maud exclaimed.

"They've never been used." Belle smoothed them lovingly. "I was keeping them till I got married."

"We'll need them this winter," Maud warned.

"I know." Belle sighed and turned back to the trunk.

The curtains were plain white muslin, with a cross-stitched blue border. Maud admired them, too. How nice it was going to be to have pretty things around. Belle herself was so pretty, even in her black dress. Dainty, too.

Maud found string and Mr. Nelson's precious store of nails to use for hanging the curtains. Belle hemmed them while Maud made biscuits for supper and fried salt pork to go with the green beans. How the day had flown! By the time they sat down to eat, the sun had set. They had to light the lamp, even though it made the room hotter and drew bugs.

Belle glanced nervously at the windows. "I'll be glad to get the curtains up, so I won't feel people can stare in at us."

"What about the door?" Maud asked. It stood wide to let out heat from the stove.

Belle smiled. "I suppose it's habit, but uncurtained windows make me feel exposed, even though they're wide open."

They had eaten and were doing the dishes when Belle gave a gasp and dropped the cup she was drying. The cup was one of the new ones. Luckily it didn't break.

"There *is* someone at the window!" Belle exclaimed. "An Indian!"

Maud felt her scalp tighten, but during the weeks she had been alone with poor sick Mr. Nelson, she had learned to conquer her fear of the dark. Indians? She'd seen small, bedraggled bands passing Kackley's farm on their way to Indian Territory, but they'd never come near the house. Without giving herself time to be frightened, she moved to the doorstep.

The waning moon lighted the freshly swept dooryard and showed the man standing against the house. For a moment Maud lost both breath and voice.

Behind her the light grew brighter. Belle had plucked the lamp from the table and was bringing it to the door.

The man stepped away from the wall, and Maud recognized him.

"Eph Coddington!" she squealed, her voice shaky from fright. "What are you doing there?"

The young man shambled into the lamplight.

"Looking to see if you was home."

"As if you didn't know when you saw the light!"

Belle put the lamp back on the table and began drying a plate as though Eph Coddington didn't exist.

"I come to tell you no hard feelings. Not on my part, anyhow." He followed Maud inside and stood looking too big for the low-ceilinged room.

"Calling after dark! I suppose you didn't think you'd frighten us by staring in the window," Maud scolded.

"No, ma'am, I didn't."

Belle went on pretending he wasn't there, so Maud had to be the one to talk to him. "Oh, sit down—do!" she said crossly. She dropped into the rocker. Eph obediently squatted on one of the kegs.

Eph wasn't as mean as his brother. Mostly just stupid. His small brown eyes peering from a bush of black hair and beard reminded Maud of buffalo she had seen—stupid, strong, and unpredictable. She offered him the two leftover biscuits and a cup of cold tea.

He accepted gratefully. "Miss Maud cooks real good." He spoke to Belle's back.

"You scared us, sneaking up like that," Maud explained.

"You two looked so purty in the lamplight, I just stopped and looked."

"Well, it's not polite. Why'd you come on foot?"

Eph swallowed and sucked his teeth. He looked more foolish than usual. "So Jake wouldn't know." He looked around. "You done something different in here."

"Yes, the carpet. Isn't it beautiful?"

"Sure is," Eph said.

Belle finished the dishwashing and stepped outside to empty the dishwater on the evening primroses that were filling the night breeze with their perfume. Eph watched the door, waiting for her to come back in.

When she reappeared, he said, "You ladies should have a dog."

"Takes money to get a dog," Maud scoffed.

"I might could get one for you." He looked hopefully at Belle.

Belle stared down her nose. "Please don't put yourself to the trouble, Mr. Coddington."

"It wouldn't be no trouble. I didn't mean to scare you, Miss—, Miss—"

"Warren," Maud supplied. She wanted to laugh. Poor Eph! Who else would come visiting when he couldn't remember the lady's name?

"I'm afraid you'll have to leave now," Belle said icily. "We've had a long day."

"Yes, ma'am." Eph stood up, looking relieved to get away. "Thanks for the biscuits," he mumbled as he clomped out the door.

Belle promptly blew out the lamp and stood in the doorway. "He's going, thank goodness!" she said after a moment. "No thanks to him I didn't fall into screaming hysterics."

"He just come to tell you no hard feelings," Maud mimicked.

The next instant they were overcome by giggles.

"Oh!" Belle gasped. "He's so awful!"

"But he's going to bring you a dog! So when he creeps up to the window, the dog will warn you!"

"Don't!" Belle gasped. "These corsets! I can't stand to laugh so hard."

"It's bedtime now, so you can take them off and laugh all you like."

"I shouldn't be laughing." Belle's voice became serious. "It's only three days since . . . since Silas died.

But so much has happened. And Silas liked to make me laugh." After a moment she said, "Does this mean they're going to leave us alone?"

"I think so!" Maud couldn't help feeling cheerful. "They're not really farmers. Jake has never planted his ten acres. Mr. Nelson thought they might be hiding out, but they go to Abilene pretty freely."

"Abilene's not overrun with lawmen," Belle said. "Let's hope they are hiding out. Then they won't want to make a stir in this neighborhood."

· 6 ·
Trail
Herd

BUT FOR BELLE, life on the claim would have fallen into familar monotony. From her trunk Belle brought calico cloth and cut out two new dresses for Maud. When Maud protested, Belle pointed out that a woman in mourning couldn't wear green or brown-and-red check.

"But you won't be wearing mourning forever," Maud said.

"The brown dress, the black and the gray will last until the year is up," Belle stated.

Maud was silenced. She had been pretending that she and Belle were settled for good. But getting two new dresses at once was so exciting that she shrugged the future away.

Belle showed her how to make finer stitches than she had thought possible. Belle on the other hand had to be taught to make bread, biscuits and cornbread.

Belle also helped hoe the garden. And in between and at night she talked about her home in Maine and read aloud from her copy of *Pilgrim's Progress*.

The days flew by, and Sunday came round almost before they knew it.

"No work today," Belle decreed at breakfast. "If we can't go to church, we can still dress up and read the Bible. What do other folks do here?" She was conscientiously trying to become a plains dweller.

"Somebody might come visiting," Maud said hopefully.

Belle raised her eyebrows.

"They'll come to see how we're getting along, and hope to be asked for dinner," Maud explained.

"Not the Coddingtons!" Belle exclaimed with a look of distaste.

Maud grinned. "The Coddingtons will be sleeping off their Saturday night in town—if they got home."

Even on Sunday one must wash breakfast dishes and sweep the floor and dooryard. That finished, Belle put on her black silk dress. Maud tied the new blue ribbons on her braids, reflecting that in another year she could wear her hair up, like Belle.

They were taking turns reading from Genesis when Charlie Dexter rode up. They invited him to read with them.

Afterwards Belle invited him to stay to dinner.

"I didn't come for that," he protested weakly. "I came to see how you're making out. Shorty Haynes told me you'd taken up the claim."

"We're going to try it for a year," Belle said. "Mr.

Nelson wanted me to stay on, and Maud's going to see if she can put up with me."

"Good for you!" Charlie exclaimed. "Money's so scarce, seems to me the best thing a person can do is get out on a good quarter section where he can get along without it."

"Is that possible?" Belle murmured.

"To get along without money?" Charlie stared across the prairie. "I surely do hope so. All I got to do is hold out four more years. Then I can borrow the cash to start farming. A lady like you won't have no trouble at all. Nothing like marrying a woman who's already got her own farm." Charlie blushed.

Belle frowned.

He said hastily, "Here, I brought you some flower seed my mother sent me." From his pocket he produced a paper packet tied with string. "I'll try to bring some antelope meat this winter, if the critters come round. There were plenty last year."

"You're very kind," Belle told him. "I'm already indebted to you for putting in Mr. Nelson's corn. Maud told me you did that."

Charlie's face turned pink again. "Glad to do it," he mumbled. "Maud more than repaid me, baking bread."

They set out the dinner—Maud with a certain pride, because it was a fancy one: beans and bread and dried apple pie, all baked the day before so that she and Belle wouldn't have to work on Sunday.

In the rocker, Charlie finished eating and sat back

with a sigh. "One of the best meals I ever ate in Kansas. I sure do thank you."

"Thank Maud," Belle said. "She cooked most of it."

Before Maud could modestly disclaim her cooking ability, she glimpsed Eph Coddington coming across the yard. "Oh-oh," she said.

He was carrying something in a dirty flour sack. When he arrived at the door and saw them sitting inside, his beard split in an embarrassed grin.

"I brung you ladies something." He held out the sack.

Maud rose to take it. It looked heavy. She guessed it was meat. The Coddingtons had probably found a stray pig last night and hadn't inquired too closely for its owner.

The sack wriggled, however, startling her so much she would have dropped it had Eph not been ready to catch it.

"What is it?" she gasped, drawing back.

He sat down in the doorstep, laid the sack on the carpet, and opened it. Out crawled a half-grown pup.

Forgetting to act grown up, Maud shrieked with delight. The pup was white, with spots of black and brown, big feet like a hound, and sharp ears like a terrier.

"I'll be gosh-derned," Charlie said.

The pup shook himself, sending off a cloud of flour dust, and made a quick tour of the room. He then headed for the door.

"Don't let him get away!" Maud screeched.

Eph blocked the pup's escape.

"Tie him up a day or two," Charlie advised. "He'll learn where he belongs."

The puppy made another tour of the room. Belle offered Eph a piece of pie. He ate it, staring at her with such obvious devotion that she flushed under her newly acquired tan. She had neither freckled nor burned. A lady's face didn't stay white out here, no matter how carefully she shielded it from the sun. The scorching wind turned everything brown. Belle's skin had acquired a warm glow that Maud thought pretty.

"How very kind of you," Belle told Eph. "Now we won't have to fear prowlers." She twinkled mischievously at Maud.

But Maud was too delighted with the gift to poke fun. "We can name him!" she exclaimed. "Is it a him?"

The men looked embarrassed. Maud felt her face grow warm. Would she never learn? Ladies didn't talk about the sex of animals!

Belle came to her rescue. "How about calling it Spot, since it has so many?"

No one showed much enthusiasm, but it got them over the awkward moment.

"It's spotted like an Indian pony, do you see?" Charlie commented, trying to agree with Belle without being obvious.

"How about Spotted Pony?" Maud asked. "There was an Indian called that. Maybe this is an Indian dog."

"Where'd you get him, Eph?" Charlie asked.

"From a fellow in town," Eph said vaguely.

No one could think of a better name, so Spotted Pony the pup became. "We can call it Spot for short," Maud offered generously.

While the ladies washed dishes, the men spliced together some harness for a dog collar and attached enough rope to tie Spotted Pony to the doorframe.

"How long will they stay?" Belle whispered.

"Till sundown, probably," Maud answered.

"My heavens, how do we entertain them?"

"I used to just sit and piece quilt blocks," Maud said. "That's kind of Sunday work."

Belle nodded. "I'll help, since I don't have anything of my own started. Next time we go to town, I'll get some thread. Would you like a crocheted collar for your green dress?"

"You can crochet!" Maud exclaimed excitedly. "Oh, please, please teach me!" During the long winter evenings one needed something interesting to do. Piecing quilt blocks grew tiresome when you had only two colors of cloth to work with.

Jake didn't come hunting his brother, and the afternoon passed pleasantly. Charlie and Belle talked politics and what the completed railroad to the Pacific would mean to the country. Eph grew bored and left. Maud suggested taking Spotted Pony for a run, but Belle shook her head, meaning she didn't want to be left alone with Charlie Dexter.

He didn't leave till sundown.

Maud made a bed of hay in the lean-to for Spotted Pony. She tied him to one of the poles holding up the brush-covered roof. He howled a bit but soon settled down.

Maud and Belle went to their separate beds almost gaily. Having a watchdog outside was a good feeling.

DURING THE DAYS that followed Spotted Pony grew so affectionate they had no fear of letting him run loose. In fact, it was only with difficulty that they kept him out of the house. In Belle's experience, dogs belonged outside. The Maine farmyard was often muddy, the wooden floors of the farmhouse spotlessly clean.

"Nothing applies here," she grumbled, adding with a reluctant laugh, "I can't object to his tracking dirt onto a dirt floor! As for a muddy yard, I'd positively welcome a little rain."

In midweek Shorty Haynes stopped with his children in the wagon to see if Belle wanted anything from town. She gave him a letter to mail to her brother. On the way back Shorty stopped to pass on a few scanty items of news. Otherwise Maud and Belle saw no one.

Maud would have been glad of a visit from her sister, but she didn't expect one. George Kackley wouldn't want his wife mixing with females living on their own. Iva might learn to stand up for herself, or slip from under his thumb.

By Sunday they were ready to welcome almost anyone.

Charlie Dexter arrived early for Bible reading, bashfully bringing a copy of the *Abilene Chronicle*. He needed little urging to stay for dinner.

Before they had finished eating, Spot began barking. Through the doorway they saw Shorty in his wagon, with Luanne and Bud on the seat beside him. Maud was glad. Now she wouldn't have to sit and listen to the adults. She and the children—Bud was nine, Luanne five—could go off and play.

Shorty took a chair made of willow withes from the back of the wagon and set it in front of Belle. "Thought maybe you could use this. I finished it last night."

Belle expressed surprise and gratitude. Maud snickered to herself. So Shorty was courting, too!

"Mr. Dexter's here," Belle was saying. "We were having pie and coffee. Will you have some?"

Shorty stepped into the soddy, looking awkward. Bud and Luanne rushed to pet the dog. Maud called them to come in for pie. They took the wedges in their hands and scurried back to the dog.

"We're going to get a kitten," Luanne announced to Maud.

Bud contradicted his sister. "All Pa said was that if he comes across one, he'll get it for you if it ain't spoke for. Let's go down to the creek."

"Can we, Maud?" Luanne seconded. "Can we go wading?"

"Ask your pa."

When asked, Shorty nodded. "But if either of you come back all muddy, you'll get a licking. I got better things to do than scrub clothes."

Luanne's dress could have done with some scrubbing, Maud noticed.

Beyond the garden the path led through tall grass down to the baked mud flat that was the rear bank of the creek where it widened out into a pool. As the water dried up and the pool shrank, the mud recorded a fascinating puzzle of footprints—raccoon, antelope, birds, skunk, and coyote. On the far side of the pool rose a limestone cliff. It went straight up, except for a narrow ledge running along its base, not far above the water. The ledge would have made a fine place to sit and fish, had there been any fish larger than minnows, or a fine place from which to dive, had the water been deeper.

Spot splashed into the water up to his belly, drank thirstily, splashed out and shook himself.

"Get away!" Maud shrieked, grabbing Luanne's hand. Laughing, they escaped all but a few drops.

"Come this way, if you want to wade." Maud led them along the bank to where the water flowed over a layer of limestone.

"This part of the pool is just like a stone floor," she called to Bud. She splashed in, holding up her skirt. "Watch it," she told Luanne. "It's slippery."

Bud rolled his pants legs to the knees, but he was soon in the water above his knees, so there was no longer any point in being careful. Soon he was wading up to his waist. Luanne's skirt got a little wet, but she was content to stay where the water was only ankle deep. Maud sat on the rocky shelf, dabbling her feet.

Nosing about at the downstream end of the pool, Spot scared up a water snake. Maud watched it swim to a crack in the limestone wall.

It was Spot who alerted her to danger. He paused in his nosing back and forth and stared up at the sweep of grass rising like a hill to the edge of the sky. With a whine he came running to Maud.

A sound of rumbling, like distant thunder, filled the quiet air, growing quickly closer. Maud heard men whooping. Even as she realized what the noise meant, the cattle came charging over the skyline, lunging through the grass, intent on water. The sun glinted on long, pointed horns. A tide of beasts poured over the brow of the prairie, galloping toward water.

Maud's first thought was to snatch Spot to keep him from running to bark at the cattle and getting trampled. Wildly she looked about. The whole herd would converge on the water hole. Those behind would push those in front until the pool was a mass of heaving brown bodies, snorting, bellowing, and—somehow— drinking water. She had seen trail herds here before, but from a distance, from the safety of Sam's back. Now—

The dry creek bed offered no escape. Cattle would come plunging down there, too. Safety lay in scrambling up onto the narrow ledge, above the clashing horns.

Maud glimpsed riders along the edge of the bawling mob pouring downhill. The cattle were being guided to the water by cowboys.

"Quick! Up here!" She swung Luanne onto the shelf and gave her a push. "Go along where it's wider. Take Spot." Luanne obeyed without question. Maud scrambled up beside her. Nearby, where the water was waist deep, Bud was trying to climb the straight-up- and-down rock. His frightened face turned up to Maud, his eyes enormous.

The first cattle were already plunging into the water.

"Your hand!" she screeched above the noise.

Luckily he was skinny as a monkey. With Maud tugging from above, his bare toes quickly found holds on the rock. He scrambled to safety and stood dripping beside her.

"Look at them!" he exclaimed. "Golly!"

Maud was looking. Now that everyone was safe above the frantic, pushing animals, she had a thought to spare for the herd itself.

"You're lucky!" Bud's voice held envy. "Tomorrow you'll have a million cow pats."

Maud was thinking the same. After the animals had drunk their fill, they would graze and rest overnight. When they moved on to Abilene tomorrow, the ground would be covered with dung. Dried, it would furnish a good part of the winter's fuel.

Suddenly Luanne began to cry. Maud turned to comfort her. "Look, that cowboy's waving his hat at us. They'll get us out somehow."

"How?" Bud demanded from between chattering teeth. He stood shivering and dripping, shifting from one foot to the other.

As Maud had foreseen, the cattle had crowded into the water and more were trying to get in. The pool surged with brown backs and tossing horns. The animals in the forefront drank their fill and fought their way out, moving upstream and down.

At the back of the herd a man Maud guessed to be the trail boss pointed to the clifftop above her head and made circling motions. He was directing two of his men to ride around to the top.

The cowboys made off upstream. Maud hoped they wouldn't take long. The flies that accompanied the herd were already buzzing hungrily about her arms and face. She knew how fiercely they bit.

Maud, Bud, and Luanne stared up at the clifftop till their necks grew uncomfortable.

"Will they pull us up?" Luanne quavered.

" 'Course they will," Bud said.

A shower of dirt and pebbles made them look up again. A pair of legs slithered over the edge. A man was being lowered, one high-heeled boot set in the rope's loop. He held the rope with one hand. With his other hand and foot he fended himself off from the rock. He hadn't even taken off his hat. Presumably the second man, above and out of sight, was paying out the rope.

The cowboy reached the ledge, took his foot from the loop, and raised his hat to Maud. "You youngsters did some quick thinking," he cried. "Hope you weren't too scared. The boss said he's sorry, he should have sent a man ahead. To tell the truth, it's been such a hard drive every man of us is too tired to think." He turned to Bud. "Think you can go up the way I came down?"

Bud nodded.

However, the cowboy had Bud slide his whole leg into the loop, so he could use both feet to keep from scraping the wall.

"Ready?"

Bud nodded, pleased to be going first.

The cowboy gave a piercing whistle, and Bud was hauled upward. He reached the top and disappeared. Soon the loop came dangling down again. Looking up, Maud saw a head in a broad-brimmed hat silhouetted against the sky.

"You next, sister," the cowboy shouted.

Maud had been puzzling how she was to put her

leg in the rope and keep her skirt modestly down at the same time. The man said, "Here, sister, you'd best sit in the loop."

"What about Luanne?"

"Is that your pretty name?" the cowboy asked.

Luanne put her finger in her mouth and hung her head.

"Don't you worry, sister," he shouted at Maud, "her and me will come up together." He widened the loop and helped Maud seat herself, then put Spot on her lap. "All right, up you go!" He gave another piercing whistle, and she began to rise.

It was a frightening trip. What if the rope broke? She saw herself falling onto all those horns. But all her concentration was needed to hold Spot and keep from being pulled against the stone face of the cliff. Her toes were getting scraped and bruised. At last a brown arm was reaching down to take Spot. Then the cowboy grasped Maud's arm and helped her over the brink. She found herself on her knees, looking into the face of a kneeling boy a year or so older than herself.

"Howdy, miss." He laughed. One of his front teeth was chipped. His face was brown from sun and dust. His red-rimmed eyes were blue. The hair of his eyebrows, eyelashes, and upper lip was dusty brown. His broad-brimmed hat, the kerchief at his throat, and his shirt—all were gray with dust. He smelled strongly of sweat and horses.

Something about his grin made Maud furious.

Before she could catch her breath to speak, however, he turned back to the work at hand. Once more the rope was lowered. Its other end was tied to the saddle horn of his pony. A second pony stood nearby, reins dragging.

Bud lay looking over the edge to watch the final act.

Maud got to her feet and smoothed her dress. She hardly had time to inspect her bruised and bleeding toes before the pony and the cowboy were straining on the rope to haul up Luanne and their rescuer. With the young cowboy's help, Luanne crawled over the edge. Bud hugged her. The pony kept the strain on the rope while the man climbed to safety. He got to his feet and began dusting his clothes with his hat while Bud stood with his arm around Luanne, waiting to see what came next.

The young cowboy grinned at Maud. "You sodbusters just about got yourselves runned over."

"You had no business trailing through here without warning!" Maud cried. It was a relief to shout at someone.

"Now, Quint, that's no way to talk to a young lady." The older man kept his hat in his hand. Where the hat had been, his forehead was pale as bacon. "The boss said we're to get these young'uns home. You take the young lady, I'll take the other two."

The boy Quint grinned again. "Never had a gal on old Star, but I'm willing to try 'er."

Maud wanted to say she'd rather walk, but the truth was her legs were shaking. She looked out over the sea of brown backs now covering the prairie. It would be a long walk; she'd have to skirt the whole herd.

Quint swung himself into the saddle and reached

for her hand. She had no choice but to let him take it. And once she'd placed her bare foot atop his booted toe, he hoisted her up. She expected him to swing her round behind him to sit a-straddle. Instead he put her in front. She found herself sitting half-sideways, one leg crooked over the horn. For somebody who'd never had a girl on his horse before, he sure knew how to go about it!

"Somebody's looking for you," he said in her ear.

From the direction of the house, Shorty Haynes's team and wagon came flying over the prairie. Charlie Dexter, on his gray, was galloping alongside.

"Pa!" Bud exclaimed from his perch behind the other cowboy.

They saw the trail boss ride to meet Shorty. All three faces turned toward the cliff. The two cowboys with the children waved their hats overhead to indicate success.

They rode down the draw to the creek bed, and up the other bank. The grazing cattle paid no attention to the riders winding their way among them.

Shorty, Charlie, and the trail boss were waiting at the chuck wagon. The cowboy set Luanne down from his horse, while Bud jumped down. She ran to her father and wrapped her arms around his leg. He picked her up and pulled her braids. Bud clutched Shorty's spare hand.

"Sorry it happened," the trail boss was saying. "Next time, I'll send a man ahead. If there is a next time. Had no idea this country was getting so settled. We got turned aside twice at gunpoint. Settlers' cows get fever, they blame us!"

Maud slid down, telling herself not to feel embarrassed. She'd never see this boy again, so there was no reason for her to feel suddenly that she was someone else.

There were no goodbyes. The boy rode off without a word. Luanne and Maud climbed into the wagon. Spot trotted beneath, safe from the hooves of cattle and horses both. Bud begged to ride on Charlie's horse, and Charlie helped him up. Once there, he looked over his shoulder and waved. She turned her head. Bud was waving to the trail boss.

Back at the house there was plenty to talk about the rest of the afternoon.

After the cuts and scrapes of the three adventurers were examined, Belle allowed herself to mention the fact that the cattle were eating her grass. The men looked embarrassed. Maud nudged her. "It's all right," she whispered. "I'll explain later."

Belle grew faintly pink.

She grew up on a farm, Maud thought. She must know cows leave cow pats. But maybe they don't need them for fuel back there.

"A herd overnighted on Martin's land last year," Shorty said enviously. "He got a drag that lasted the family all winter."

"A drag?" Belle murmured, fearful of asking another wrong question.

Charlie welcomed something he could talk about without blushing. "A drag can't keep up. Some outfits give them away. Others hate homesteaders so bad they'd rather feed the drags to coyotes."

· 7 ·

Quint
Farwell

MAUD'S FIRST THOUGHT next morning was of Sam. In all the excitement, she had forgotten the horse. It would be a disaster if he got mixed with the Texans' string of spare horses. Not that they'd mean to include him—that would be horse-stealing, the worst crime on the frontier—but one had an obligation to look after one's stock, too. Someone would have to go after him. Without a horse, she'd have to ask one of the neighbors to fetch him.

Maud was pulling her dress over her head when Spot began to bark. She came out of her curtained-off bedroom to find Belle already dressed and ordering Spot to hush.

The visitor was one of the cowboys. He stepped into the smooth-swept dooryard and raised his hat. The trail boss!

"Howdy, ma'am. Could I speak to the man of the house?"

"There isn't one," Belle said frostily.

"Oh—" He scratched his head. "Well, maybe two ladies is better. One of our boys has broke his leg."

Belle gave an exclamation of dismay.

"We could take him to Abilene in the chuck wagon, but we'd have to find someone there to take care of him. We was thinking he'd be more comfortable if we left him here, with a family, if you have someplace to put him. We'd leave beef and flour for his keep."

"But—" Belle began, "how long—?" She looked doubtfully at Maud, who knew what she was thinking. How could they take in a strange man—maybe a rough and dirty one who'd gone to Texas to escape his misdeeds? The beef and flour would be a godsend, though.

"I ought to explain, ma'am—" The man read their thoughts. "It's the boy. I wouldn't ask you to take one of the toughs. This is young Farwell. He's what—no more than sixteen. He's an orphan, except for his brother. A little home life wouldn't hurt him."

Maud's heart gave a thump. Quint Farwell, that had been the boy's name! She'd never expected to see him again.

"Well, I guess we could—" Belle looked distracted, but Maud was overjoyed. Beef, flour, and all the excitement of an unexpected guest.

Belle asked, "Will you send someone for the doctor?"

"His brother already rode to Abilene, ma'am. Even if we took the boy to town, we couldn't jolt him all that way with his leg unset. If it's all right with you, then, I'll have him brought up."

Belle gave a flustered glance round the room. "Has he had breakfast?"

The man's eyes squinted. He looked amused. "Yes, ma'am, couple of hours ago, before he broke his leg. The herd's on the move. We cut out your horse—if it was yours?"

"I was just going to look for him!" Maud exclaimed.

The boss nodded to Belle. "I sure want to thank you, ma'am. The cook'll bring the supplies." He glanced at the sun. "I'll be getting along." Setting his hat on his head, he turned toward his horse.

Belle drew breath, as though to call after him, then gave Maud a baffled look. "I guess there's nothing more to say. I'll give him my bed and move in with you."

"Goody!" Maud was not fond of sleeping alone. Another person in the soddy was going to make things so much cozier.

Belle readied the bed. Maud built the fire so they could get breakfast out of the way. They had barely finished their cornbread and molasses when they heard the wagon. They hurried out to meet it.

The cook was short, fat, and whiskery. He climbed down from the wagon and went round to the back. He was strong, too. He pulled Quint from the end of the canvas-covered wagon and threw him over his shoulder as though he were a sack of flour. Quint's boots had been removed; his feet were bare, and he was perfectly limp. He looked slimmer, more boyish than he had on the back of a horse.

The man deposited him on the bed and went out. Quint lay lifeless, eyes closed. His face was greenish under his tan. His brown hair hung lank. One bare ankle was swollen horribly.

Maud looked fearfully at Belle.

"He's fainted from the pain," Belle said. "It would have been monstrous to jolt him all the way to Abilene!"

The cook reappeared in the doorway with a pair of boots in one hand and a sack of flour over his shoulder.

"Where you want this?" he asked.

"On that box for now," Belle directed. The flour bin under the bed was half-full. They'd have to think of a place to put the extra bag where it would be safe from mice and damp.

The cook dumped the flour and boots, went out again, and returned with a side of beef. He dropped that on the table and removed his hat.

"What about the boy's clothes?" Belle asked.

The man looked surprised. "He don't have spare clothes, ma'am. We aim to buy a change in Abilene."

"I see."

The cook stood holding his hat. "Ma'am, the boss said to tell you, he's leaving you one of the drags. She calved last night. She's old, but she come through it. She needs rest, much as anything."

"A cow!" Maud gasped. She struggled for words to thank him. Belle, too, appeared speechless.

"The boss is sorry the herd scared your young'uns,"

the cook explained. "She's tied to the big cottonwood tree. She ain't tame, understand."

Before Maud could do more than gasp thank you, he was gone.

Belle was looking stunned. "Is he leaving us to revive the boy?"

"Looks that way," Maud said happily. The amazing gift of a cow made Quint's arrival take second place. And meat and flour! Belle would be bound to like homesteading better if they didn't run short of food come winter.

A new worry smote her. "Belle, I don't know how to milk!"

"I do," Belle said, her eyes on the boy. She sniffed. Inside the small room, their visitor smelled strongly unwashed.

"He's got to be bathed," she said firmly. "Then we can put him into one of Silas's nightshirts." Mr. Nelson's clothes had been washed and laid away against whatever need.

The boy stirred.

"He's coming around," Maud pointed out.

Quint looked at them from pain-blurred eyes. "Where am I?"

"In my home," Belle told him. "The doctor's on his way. We're going to look after you till you can walk again."

"They left me?"

"Your boss thought a wagon trip would be too hard."

"I remember. My brother went for the doctor."

"That's right. Would you like a cup of coffee."

"Thank you, ma'am, I would. I hope you won't take offense, ma'am, but I can't stay here, taking you folks's bed."

"I'm afraid you must," Belle told him. "Till your bone knits. I assure you, you're not imposing. There are only two of us, and we have another bed."

"Your boss give us a cow and a calf," Maud put in. "Besides this hunk of beef."

For the first time Quint noticed her. He managed a lopsided grin. "I hope I'm worth it."

"All right if I go look at her?" Maud asked Belle.

"You might bring a bucket of water first." She followed Maud outside. "Maybe the doctor will bathe him."

Maud fetched the water, then skipped lightheartedly down the path, ignoring the dew-wet grass. Her skirt clung wetly to her legs, but she pushed eagerly on.

The big cottonwood grew on the creek bank. It had been scarred by lightning and scorched by prairie fire. Half its broad trunk was stripped of bark.

Maud couldn't see the cow at first. Had it escaped and wandered away, its calf following? Then she saw it, lying down, chewing its cud, grateful for the rest after its long, burdened walk from Texas. As Maud approached, it lurched to its feet—a skinny, rangy creature, all head and long black horns.

"So-o-o, bossy! So-o, boss," she said. Her voice held laughter. The idea that these words, meant for the friendly family cow, would soothe this wild critter! Still, a cow was a cow, and could be tamed. Good luck that Belle could milk. They would have to tame the cow before the calf grew old enough for its mother to wean it. If Belle could be milking the cow by then, she could probably go on milking it till spring. If it had plenty to eat.

"I'll start cutting hay," Maud said aloud. "Enough for both you and Sam."

The cow was still on her feet, head lowered, as though daring Maud to approach. The calf struggled to stand on spindly legs and began sucking noisily.

Maud sat on the ground where the early-morning shade of the cottonwood crossed the path. She went on talking.

"We might as well start getting acquainted. Because you're mine, now. Ours, really, but Belle's not as excited about you as I am. I'll be the one to look after you."

The cow switched her burr-filled tail. Suddenly she said, "Moo-oo!" so loudly Maud jumped. Then she tossed her head, took her gaze off Maud, and lay back down.

"Poor thing!" Maud exclaimed. "You've walked a long ways, haven't you? And now they've tied you where you can't reach the water."

The cow was indeed tied by a short rope. Maud's heart thudded. In order to add more rope, someone would have to get quite close to those horns. Who?

It didn't seem fair to ask help from Charlie or Shorty. Of course, if one of them happened to stop by—

She could ask Quint! He could tell her if it was safe to approach a Texas cow.

"The first thing to do," she told the animal, "is bring you a bucket of water." Mr. Nelson had a big wooden bucket made of staves, like a barrel. Maud fairly danced back up the path to the house, happy to do something for the cow. She carried the heavy bucket to the spring, filled it, and set it before the cow. With satisfaction Maud watched the animal rise and drink deeply.

Then she said, "I could name you. Belle won't mind. How would you like to be called Lady? But you'd have to act like one."

Two horseflies came buzzing round. It was time to move on.

Maud found Sam grazing among the sunflowers, spoke a few friendly words to him, and started back toward the house. On the way she surveyed the night's droppings of cow dung. They were all over the place! When they had dried, she would gather them and stack them beside the lean-to. They looked like enough to last all winter.

The doctor had not arrived, but Quint seemed to be sleeping. Maud described the cow, but didn't mention the short rope.

She and Belle had another big chore ahead—drying the meat. Maud went back to the creek with the axe and cut saplings to make a drying rack.

Last summer an old settler from down on the Arkansas River had stopped overnight at Kackley's. He had told Iva how the Indians dried buffalo meat, and Maud had helped her sister dry some beef. One made a rack like two wide ladders propped against each other and hung the strips of meat to dry in the sun and wind. After a few days the meat became like leather. It would keep for months. Boiled with a little wild onion and potatoes or cornmeal, it made a good meal.

Maud had cut poles and was tying them together when the doctor arrived. He brought with him an old sheet and neatly sawn splints. While he drank a cup of tea, Belle and Maud tore the sheet into bandages.

When everything was ready, the doctor spoke to Quint and took his pulse. Quint groaned and opened his eyes. From a flask the doctor filled a cup half-full of whisky. He made Quint drink it. Then he set his leg.

Before it was over, Quint fainted from the pain. The doctor didn't bring him round until he had the leg bandaged. Then he helped Belle put Quint into a nightshirt and told her to let him sleep. When Quint felt better, he could bathe himself. Belle had to be satisfied with putting Quint's dirty clothes outside till they could be washed.

She gave the doctor boiled beef for dinner with new potatoes from the garden.

"I didn't think much of that boy's brother," Doc Owen said. "Strange how sometimes you take a man in dislike on a hunch. He had shifty eyes."

The phrase struck Maud. That was the trouble with the Coddingtons! Jake had shifty eyes. Eph never looked you straight in the face, either, but his look was more hangdog than shifty.

When Doc Owen left, they gave him a chunk of meat to pay for his visit. He promised to ride out again in about two weeks.

Maud and Belle spent the rest of the afternoon cutting meat into strips and hanging it on the rack while Spot howled from the lean-to where he had to be tied to keep him from dragging the strips away and burying them.

Quint woke toward evening. The sickly green look was gone. Belle had bathed his face and neck and wiped the dust from his hair. He wanted to get up, but when he discovered he was wearing a nightshirt, he blushed and changed his mind.

Taking pity on him, Belle got out a pair of Silas's trousers and opened a seam so Quint could get them over his bound leg. Then they propped him up so he could eat supper with them.

At first he was shy, barely replying to questions. Belle asked him about the accident.

"The pony put his foot in a hole," he said.

"Was he hurt?" Maud asked.

"I don't think so."

"Don't you *know?*" Maud was aghast. "Don't you care about your horse?"

"He wasn't mine, just one of the string. If I remember right, he scrambled up and waited for me to climb back aboard. Then everything went black."

"Well, we're very glad to have you here," Belle said.

"And the cow!" Maud added.

"Did the doc say how long I'd be laid up, ma'am?"

"I didn't think to ask!" Belle exclaimed. "He said he'd stop by to see how you were coming along."

"You mean I've got to wear this till he drops in?" Quint's shyness was wearing off fast.

"It was six weeks when my brother broke his leg—"

"They'll be going back before then!" Quint interrupted. "Didn't the boss say *anything?*"

"I expect he wasn't looking that far ahead." Belle smiled gently.

"I suppose I could ride in the chuck wagon." Quint made a face. "I'm sorry to be crowding you folks."

"You're not," Belle told him. "We have plenty of room."

Quint looked unbelieving. "Your husband might think different."

"He might"— Belle's eyes saddened —"if I had one. As it is, I'm boss."

"You run this place?"

"There isn't much to run."

"Are you—what do they call it—homesteading this land?" He grinned, showing his chipped tooth.

"That's right. Maud and I are qualified sod-busters."

"Well," Quint said. "I guess maybe I'm *not* in the way. Maybe you need a man around."

Maud felt herself swelling with indignation. He was talking as though Belle were the only person in the room. Besides, what good could he do—laid up with a busted leg? She remembered she wanted to question him.

"Then you can tell us what to do about the cow," she said.

"Do about her?" He laughed.

"I want to untie her and make her rope longer."

"Don't you farmers know how to handle a cow?" His voice was scornful.

"Not Texas cows." Maud put up with his scorn because she needed the information.

"Oh, my!" Belle was exclaiming. "Does she have long horns?"

"Lasso her," Quint said. He looked back at Belle,

his blue eyes softened. "Be careful you don't get hurt, ma'am."

I'm the one who'll get hurt, Maud thought indignantly. "Then what?" she asked.

He took his gaze off Belle to say, "Slip a noose over one horn and tie her head to something. Then come up from behind and untie the other rope. Look out she doesn't kick."

Gloomily Maud watched him finish his supper. She could see already that he wasn't going to be the least bit friendly or fun to have around.

Belle was eyeing her. "That sounds dangerous."

Maud shrugged. She wasn't going to let this Texas boy know she was scared of a cow. The trouble was, there wasn't any spare rope. Rope was expensive. She wondered if Charlie or Shorty had any. She wouldn't ask the Coddingtons for anything. The cook had dumped Quint's saddle in the lean-to. His rope might be with it.

It was still daylight when they finished eating. Quint lay back and closed his eyes.

Maud said in an undertone, "I'm going to see if Lady's got water. Do you like Lady for a name?"

"In the hope that she'll behave like one?"

"Yes." Maud smiled.

Belle followed her outside.

Maud said, "I need to find some rope. Lady's tether is too short to let her eat."

"Poor thing," Belle said. "You'll be careful about getting close to her, won't you?"

Maud promised, and Belle said, "What do you think of Quint?"

Maud made a face. "He's all right, for a boy."

Belle laughed. "I think you've hit the nail on the head."

She went back inside, and Maud went to look at Quint's saddle. The rope coiled over the saddle horn was made of fine hemp, tightly twisted and flexible. It looked clean and oiled. It looked, in other words, too good to use as a tether. She'd have to go borrowing. Quint's rope would do, however, to tie Lady's head while another piece was added to the tether she had. Then she could be fastened to a stake and eat in a circle all around it.

Both cow and calf were lying down when Maud arrived to refill the water bucket. They should be brought in overnight, Maud thought, in case coyotes came round. The way the cow was tied, she wouldn't be able to use her horns to protect the calf.

For once, Sam came when Maud whistled. She swung herself onto his bare back. Guiding him with her knees, she rode across the prairie to the Haynes' place.

Shorty was sitting in the yard smoking his pipe. Inside Bud and Luanne were doing dishes and quarreling.

Maud told him the news and explained her errand.

"How come I didn't get no cow?" Shorty said. "They scared my kids, too."

"I guess Belle would like you to have some of the meat," Maud offered.

"I was only teasing!" Shorty exclaimed. "Who's going to milk her?"

"Belle can milk," Maud said.

"You tell her to be careful," Shorty advised. "Tell

her not to be in any hurry. Give the cow plenty of time to tame up."

He searched the rafters of his one-room house and the shed. "I thought I had a spare length. I guess I used it."

Maud said she'd try Charlie. Bud begged to go along.

"If it's all right with your pa," Maud said. Shorty nodded.

So the two of them jogged to Charlie's. He, too, was sitting in his dooryard.

"By gum," he said, "I was just a-wishing some human being would come along—and here are two of you."

Maud explained her errand and told Charlie about their new boarder. She was in luck. Charlie not only had rope to spare, but he offered to come along and help, to Maud's relief.

He saddled his mare and they set out, stopping at Shorty's to set Bud down.

They stopped for Maud to get Quint's lasso from the lean-to, and then she and Charlie rode on down to the creek in the fading light.

With Charlie's help, things went smoothly. The cow came to her feet. Charlie rode up and dropped the noose over one horn. He pulled it taut. The calf saw a chance to get its supper.

Maud dismounted and talked soothingly to the cow while she untied the rope from around the cottonwood and lengthened it with the piece Charlie had lent her.

"All right," Charlie shouted. "See if you can lead her up to the house. If she tries to charge you, I'll hold her back. If she takes a notion to go after me, let go your rope. Brownie can run faster than she can."

"Come, Lady," said Maud. "You're going to your barn, where you'll be safe, and so will—" The calf had no name. Good, Belle could name him.

The cow walked into the lean-to and allowed herself to be tied to one of the poles in the most docile way possible.

"Don't let her fool you," Charlie warned. "She's tired. Tomorrow or the day after may be another story."

Belle heard them and came out to greet Mr. Dexter. It was almost too dark to see anything, but the cow's horns glinted. It was the first time Belle had been close to a Texas cow.

"Mercy!" she exclaimed. "If I'd known it had horns like that, I'd never have let you go near. I don't know how you can be so pleased about something so dangerous."

"You just have to be careful, ma'am." Charlie said. "If she don't get gentle, you can always eat her."

"If she doesn't eat us first!"

"Anyhow," Maud began, "the calf is a—" She stopped and caught her breath. She had been about to say *bull*, but it wasn't a word ladies used. "The calf still doesn't have a name," she said quickly.

"We'll name it later," Belle agreed. "I'm sorry I can't ask you to sit and visit awhile, Mr. Dexter, but Quint's asleep."

"I just come to give Maud a hand," Charlie said. "I've got to get back and shut up my poultry." Charlie had bought five goose eggs in the spring, and his old hen had hatched them. So far the goslings had all survived.

Like Mr. Nelson's chickens, they had their own little sod house at night, in which they stayed safe from coyotes and weasels.

"You can't say this hasn't been an exciting day," Belle remarked while she and Maud undressed in the dark. "But now I'm wondering how to entertain him."

· 8 ·
Troubles

"WHY DOES he have to be entertained?" Maud asked next morning. She and Belle were in the lean-to, looking at the cow and calf by daylight.

"I didn't mean *entertain*, exactly. I meant something to keep him busy. What about lessons? It would give you a chance to brush up, too."

"I'll bet he can't even write his name," Maud said loftily. "What if he doesn't want to learn?"

"I think he'll want to." Belle's lips curved in a confident smile. Maud understood the meaning of that smile. Quint hadn't been there twenty-four hours, yet already he was so sweet on Belle he'd do anything she asked. Not that Maud cared the least little bit. The cow had come because of him. Because of the cow, when she could be milked, Belle's money would last longer. They could make butter and might trade it for other things.

And if Belle got to teaching Quint, perhaps she'd have courage enough to apply for the school job. If she had a job, she'd feel rooted here, would want to stay on. Today was the first of August. It was time Belle went to talk to Mr. Randolph.

Rather fearfully they untied the cow. Belle held the long lasso rope and Maud held the rope that was tied around Lady's neck. Somehow they coaxed and tugged her down to the spring to drink and then tied her to a sapling. It was a struggle. Dew soaked their skirts. Belle's sunbonnet slipped off and twisted round her neck.

"Oh, dear," she panted. "Do we have to look forward to this morning and night? We won't have the strength left to milk her."

The calf seemed healthy and frisky. And Maud knew the cow would soon look better, too. Maybe she'd tame down. They'd have to hope so.

They walked back up the slope to the high prairie, and Belle suddenly laughed. "My, what a sense of accomplishment!"

The morning was still pleasantly cool. Insects hummed in the sparkling grass. The wind was gentle.

"What a lovely time of day," Belle said.

"It is!" Maud was always pleased when Belle said she liked something. The future seemed more secure then.

Maud's first job every morning was to let the chickens out. Now as they passed the chicken house, one of the hens began to cackle.

"An egg!" Maud exclaimed.

Mr. Nelson had laid up some sods to make a nest

in one corner of the chicken house. There atop the sods lay a white egg.

"The first one!" Maud exulted. "When we get milk and butter from the cow, we can have pancakes."

She passed the egg to Belle, who said, "Yes, indeed. Meanwhile this egg will taste good in the cornbread."

Quint was awake and hungry. Belle had left mush cooking on the stove. Soon they were all at breakfast.

"Lessons!" Quint growled when Belle suggested them. "Are you a schoolteacher?"

"Yes. Isn't that fortunate?"

"I'm no schoolboy. Taking a herd on the trail is a man's job."

"I'm sure it is," Belle agreed. "But I've been wondering how you're to pass the time. There's very little else for you to do."

"I've got my knife. I could whittle some bowls and stuff."

"The wood around here isn't good for whittling." Maud said. "It's cottonwood."

"This prairie don't seem to have much of nothin'." Quint sneered.

Maud was feeling too good-tempered this morning to quarrel. "Shorty Haynes might have some elm," she offered.

"Whittling doesn't sound like a twelve-hour occupation," Belle said.

"We could always talk." Quint grinned. "I could sit and chat with ladies for hours."

"Then you won't mind if our talk is in the form of lessons."

Quint glowered. He indicated Maud with his head. "What does she do all day?"

"This morning she's going to help me wash clothes," Belle answered. "This afternoon I'm going to see how well you both spell."

AT THE POOL by the springs they poured soft soap over the wet clothes and beat them on the smooth limestone rock. By the time they finished, the sun had climbed high. The sparse trees no longer furnished shade.

"He's had time to get bored and lonesome," Belle said. "Why don't you go back and start dinner. I'll come along when I've washed my hair."

Quint was sitting up in bed, reading one of Belle's magazines. Maud felt suddenly shy at finding herself alone with him.

"Belle will be up in a while," she said. She built a fire and began to fry last night's meat and potatoes. She hoped Belle wouldn't take too long.

She was laying the table when Quint suddenly threw down the magazine.

"I guess a feller ought to take advantage of the chance for schooling," he offered.

Maud was tonguetied.

"I suppose you're in the eighth grade," Quint said.

Without looking at him, Maud said she was.

"Girls don't have anything better to do," he taunted.

She was spurred to say, "I suppose you have!"

"I *had* a job. Anybody can get his leg broke. I'll still get most of my pay."

If things had turned out differently, Maud thought, she might now be working in town. But then she couldn't finish school. She wouldn't have Belle. Quint wouldn't be there, either.

Belle came in at last, her wet hair braided and coiled round her head. They gathered round the table.

When grace had been said, Quint announced his decision. "I've thought it over, ma'am. If you're willing to teach me, I'd be dumb not to let you."

"And you're not dumb," Belle concluded. "What was your last grade in school?"

"Uh, the sixth—sort of. In St. Louis. Then my mother—uh—died, and Verne and me went to Texas."

"Is your father dead, too?" Belle asked gently.

"Yes, ma'am. Killed in the War."

"How old were you when you went to Texas?"

"Going on eleven. Old enough to do a day's work."

"And too young to understand the value of an education," Belle said.

Quint looked doubtful.

"Someday you will," Belle pursued.

"Speaking of education, ma'am"—Quint's grin showed his broken tooth—"who's going to milk that cow?"

"I suppose I am." Belle sounded reluctant.

"How do we tame her?" Maud coaxed.

Quint grinned at them. "Guess you ladies could use some lessons, too," he said with infuriating smugness.

"Not with your leg," Belle reminded him.

"You don't know, either!" Maud prodded.

"No, I don't," he admitted. "I guess I'd just keep trying. First of all, you should take her calf away. Can you pen it in the lean-to here?"

Maud nodded.

Belle said, "That means we'll have to listen to it bawling all day, but I guess I can stand it."

"There's no other way," Quint said.

"I know," Belle agreed.

"I'd bring the cow up in the evening," Quint went on, "and tie her head to a post and put a rope around her back legs so she can't kick you. The calf can take his supper from one side while you milk from the other. Then I'd tie her near the house overnight and do the same thing in the morning. She ought to get used to the idea after a few days, if you can keep from upsetting her."

"That will take some doing," Belle said.

To Maud it sounded impossible, but Belle had nodded agreement with Quint's method. They all rose from the table with the friendly feeling of having shared a problem. Quint began to seem like a member of the household.

Next morning Maud cut saplings and built a pen across one side of the stable. After a struggle she and Belle shut the calf into it. By the end of a day of listening to it bawl for its mother, Maud wasn't sure she wanted milk that badly.

When evening came Belle got half a cupful. It tasted so good in the coffee that Maud grew hard-hearted. Nothing was hurting the calf; it was simply lonesome. And besides, Belle would like homesteading better if they had milk.

The lessons turned out to be rather enjoyable, more like a family than a school. Quint was more or less confined to his bed, though he sometimes sat on the floor beside the door, with his back against the wall and his legs stretched out on the rug. Over his shoulder he could see the yard and the shimmering prairie.

The meat was dried and stored in wooden boxes under Quint's bed, so Spot was free to come and go. He liked to curl up in the dust right outside the door, where Quint could reach out and scratch his ears.

Maud did her studying wherever she liked. Sometimes she took her list of spelling words to the creek and spelled aloud to Lady until the flies drove her away. Sometimes she read at the table, where the hot wind blowing through the open door stirred the hot air.

They were thus occupied one hot afternoon, and Belle was sewing, when Mr. Randolph rode up. He was the man whose say-so hired the teacher. No doubt he had heard about Belle.

Maud performed introductions. Mr. Randolph accepted a cupful of cold well water. While he drank it, Maud pointed out that she and Quint were studying.

Mr. Randolph didn't appear interested.

"Miss Warren," he said, when he got up to leave, "I wonder if I might speak privately."

Belle walked with him to where his horse was tethered. Quint and Maud were left to stare at each other.

"He's going to ask her to teach school," Maud whispered.

"Think so?" Quint muttered.

Maud bit her lip and stared out the door. "She just has to get the job."

After a moment Maud heard his horse going away, and Belle stepped into the room. "Don't be disappointed. He didn't come to offer me the school. He wants to buy the land."

"*Buy* it! Your claim?"

"Yes. He said it can be done. Of course, I said I wasn't interested."

"He's got enough land!" Maud exclaimed.

"I asked him about the school." Belle frowned. "He said he'd let me know."

Evenings after sundown they sat outside, enjoying the cooler air, the feeling of security as night closed in, blotting out the immensity of sky and land, bringing their circle down to soddy, lean-to, and dancing fireflies.

One night a red glow shone on the southern horizon. Maud pointed it out. "Prairie fire."

The grass was drying and curing where it stood. Sam and Lady and the calf could eat from it all winter. Only a small haystack would be needed to last through storms, and Maud was working on that.

Blown by the wind, however, fire could sweep across the dried grass with the speed of runaway horses.

The day after the glow appeared, Mr. Martin came with his team of mules. With a wave toward the house, he began replowing the weed-choked square around the yard and house.

"That's the fire guard," Maud explained. "If a fire comes, it won't leap over plowed ground—we hope."

"How can we repay him?" Belle worried. "If only we could get more than a cupful of milk from the cow!"

The mules went round and round; the strip of plowed earth grew wider.

"The dried beef?" Maud suggested.

Belle shook her head. In her eyes the meat was for Quint.

"Go ahead, use some of it," Quint said.

Instead Belle opened her big trunk and surveyed the folded garments.

"Silas would be glad for me to use his clothes," Belle said.

Maud agreed.

They offered Mr. Martin the remaining pair of Silas's trousers. At first he refused, saying he was simply being neighborly, but Belle said if he didn't take them, the moths would. He left with the trousers carefully wrapped round the stretcher between the plow handles.

Maud felt secure every time she looked at the wide fireguard, but till a path was trampled, walking over freshly plowed earth was a nuisance when she went to the garden or fetched the cow.

As THE DAYS WENT BY Lady became used to the idea of being milked. They began to have more milk than they could use before it soured, but of course there were uses for sour milk—butter and pancakes and cottage cheese.

Grasshoppers had been troublesome all summer, thudding this way and that every time a person walked through the grass, but late one afternoon while Quint and Maud were quietly working at their assigned lessons, the sunlight dimmed.

Maud looked up from her book. "There must be a storm coming!" She hurried to the door.

Belle laid aside her sewing. Quint swung his legs over the side of the bed.

"It looks more like dust," Maud puzzled.

"Too small for a duststorm," Quint said, looking over her head.

"A fire?" Belle asked, never having seen a prairie fire.

Quint and Maud shook their heads.

The cloud was nearer than it first appeared. It shimmered and swirled, glittering like snowflakes, with a sound like a muffled roar. The roar grew and grew until suddenly the prairie was pelted with heavy raindrops. But it wasn't rain, it was grasshoppers.

From the doorway they watched in astonishment. The hens began darting this way and that.

"It's raining grasshoppers!" Maud screeched. One flew in her face. Another landed on her head.

"They're coming inside," Belle shrieked. "Shut the door!"

With the door and windows shut, the room became stiflingly hot. Quint peered through the window above his bed. Maud and Belle looked through the other window. The dooryard crawled and jumped with insects, and still they dropped from the sky and thudded against the door.

"I read about this back East," Belle said, "but it was so unbelievable—"

"The garden!" Maud cried, snatching her sunbonnet from the peg.

"I'll come with you," Belle said.

As they ran out the door, they heard Quint cursing his useless leg.

"This never happened here before," Maud gasped, feeling the grasshoppers crunch under her bare heels.

Belle had been going barefoot, too, these last days. Now she squealed and hopped, but she kept running.

More grasshoppers were in the garden than anywhere, if possible. They were eating the small onions Maud had grown so carefully from seed, and the turnips, the green pumpkins, the winter squash. They swarmed over tomato and cucumber vines.

Maud and Belle pulled onions and turnips as fast as they could, filling their aprons and hurrying back to the house. Tiny bloody scratches appeared on Belle's face. Maud felt her own face, arms, and legs getting scratched, too, by barbs on the creatures' legs.

Maud saw Spot eat one, and then another and another. The sight made her feel like throwing up, but she had no time to be squeamish. The hens were pecking away like mad things.

The girls flew into the house, dumped their load of vegetables on the table, and rushed out again, pausing only to tell Quint what was going on. He had reopened the door and windows and was limping about, collecting the insects that came in, grinding them under his heel.

"You're making the house messy!" Maud screeched at him on her second trip.

"What do you want me to do with them?"

"Throw them in the stove!"

"There's no fire."

"Build one. Ugh, they're in the water bucket!"

Quint paused in his hobbling. "What about the well?"

Maud stared at him.

"Cover it with something—a quilt," Quint directed.

The quilts were stored for the summer beneath Quint's mattress. He helped Maud haul one out and she rushed outdoors.

Mr. Nelson had been proud of his well. It was framed round with wood, like a box, and had a windlass over the top, so the bucket didn't have to be pulled up hand over hand. Grasshoppers were dropping into the well at the same rate as they were falling on the ground. Maud flung the quilt over the opening.

What about the corn—the young ears with their soft, milky kernels? Maud ran to the cornfield through a shower of grasshoppers dropping from the sky and crunching under foot. The green field looked as though it had sprouted some new disgusting kind of growth. Grasshoppers covered every leaf and stalk. The thousands of crunching jaws made a low humming that filled the air. Maud's stomach churned. The sickness in her middle became a solid thing, like a stone. The corn was what they had depended on to see them through the winter. Without that—

But there wasn't time to think so far ahead.

Maud ran back to the garden. Belle had pulled the

turnips and tossed them in a pile. At least that way the ones underneath would be protected till they could be carried into the house.

The potatoes were far enough underground to be safe.

Maud returned to the house with a green pumpkin under each arm. Maybe they would ripen inside. Then she ran again to the well, thinking that if too many grasshoppers landed on the quilt, the sheer weight might make quilt and all fall in. The quilt was still there. The grasshoppers were eating the wool! With a howl of anger she snatched up the quilt and tried to shake the grasshoppers onto the ground.

"They're eating the quilt!" she cried, rushing it back into the house.

"It's probably too late anyway," Quint drawled. "I wish I could do something besides sit here and think about what all they're eating."

That evening they didn't sit outside. The ravenous grasshoppers didn't quiet down until darkness fell. Indoors was hot, but at least the house wasn't crawling with insects. Belle sat in the rocking chair. Maud, on one of the kegs, leaned her elbows on the table. Quint was propped up in bed. The moon came up, and light streamed through the windows.

After a while Maud made herself say, "They got the corn, too." After this calamity Belle might not even want to stay the winter.

Belle looked as though she didn't understand the doom in Maud's voice.

"We won't have cornmeal for the winter," Maud explained.

"Oh." Belle's tired mind seemed to have trouble making the connection.

"What are we going to do?" Maud wailed, bringing their plight into the open. "We'll have to *buy* cornmeal. Come spring, you'll have to buy seed corn, too. I guess you won't want to stay after this?"

"I have to stay for a year," Belle stated. "It was Silas's dying wish. I went against my brother's advice in coming here, and then I wrote him and bragged about my land. If I'm given the schoolteaching job, we'll be all right."

"The water won't be fit to drink," Quint said quietly.

Belle disagreed. "We can use it if it's boiled. It may taste terrible, but it won't poison us."

"We can get drinking water from the spring," Maud reminded them.

"Then why shouldn't we stay?" Belle demanded. "This is our home! This year, at any rate."

Maud wriggled. "They're just so disgusting!"

Quint said, "Except for the corn, how much worse off will you be?"

"They've ruined the whole garden! And the water. Isn't that enough?" Maud spoke angrily, glad he'd raised an argument.

"The garden wouldn't have lasted much longer."

"It might have rained."

"Sure, and the sky might fall, too," Quint scoffed. "All you've really lost is your corn. The water will be kind of tainted, but as you say, you can get drinking water from the creek."

"My onions," Maud mourned.

Belle said, "If that's the worst of our troubles, I agree with Quint—we're pretty lucky."

"Sure," he said. "You'll have grass for the animals. If you get the teaching job—"

"*If*," Maud echoed under cover of darkness. In the months she had looked after Mr. Nelson, she had had to be cheerful so many times in the face of near disaster that now she took a twisted pleasure in voicing her frightened thoughts.

"I'll go see Mr. Randolph as soon as these creatures leave," Belle promised.

Maud understood that going to Mr. Randolph wasn't quite the thing to do. If a schoolteacher lived at home, a member of the school board usually approached her father. But since Belle didn't have a father, and she wanted the job—

"I'm going to try cutting hay when the 'hoppers are gone," Quint announced. "I've sharpened your sickle. I figure I can sit on the ground and swing it. After it dries, all you'll have to do is load the wagon and build the stack."

"All!" Maud echoed. She knew she ought to be grateful for Quint's offer. She ought to be glad that Belle was not going to let the grasshoppers drive them away, but she felt wretched. She felt like going to bed and covering her head. But it was simply too hot. . . .

THE GRASSHOPPERS stayed for two days. They ate everything except the prairie grass and the row of castor beans. They ate the leaves off the cottonwood trees along Dry Creek. They crept into the house and ate holes in the hanging clothes and the carpet. On the morning of the third day, the wind changed to the west. All at once the creatures took wing and flew away. "To plague someone else," Belle reminded Quint and Maud when they would have celebrated.

There was really nothing to celebrate. Charlie Dexter stopped on his way to town and again on his way home. He brought the Abilene paper. Belle invited him for supper. Maud put the meal on the table while Belle read the news aloud.

They learned that many people were worse off than they themselves. Most homesteaders had counted on selling corn to buy the other things they needed.

"Folks are leaving," Charlie said. "I seen dozens of wagons heading east. I may have to go back to Iowa and look for a job myself to tide me over."

So much for his promises of meat, Maud thought. He won't be here to do any hunting.

BUT IT WAS ALMOST impossible to think of winter. Day after day the heat and drought continued. The wild grass turned dry and sand-colored in the hot wind. To a hawk circling above the prairie, the land must indeed look like a great desert. At night when they sat outside to cool off, the sky was often red in one direction or another. That meant that twenty or twenty-five miles away a prairie fire was burning and would go on burning unchecked until it reached a stream or some other natural barrier.

"I wonder sometimes who ever thought this country could be tamed," Belle said one evening. "I can understand why they wanted to. Not a stone or a stump, and all this rich black earth."

Maud and Quint could recall only vaguely any other kind of country. What did Belle mean by "tame country"?

Hot day succeeded hot day. The nights were hardly cooler. No neighbors stopped by. It was too hot to do anything but stay in the shade and wait for sundown.

The lessons continued. Studying helped Maud keep her mind off the heat.

Late one afternoon Doc Owen appeared. He was afoot, leading his horse. "Too hot to ride," he explained when Maud met him outside the house.

"Have you come to take the splints off?" was Quint's first question.

"No chance of that," Doc said cheerfully. "I was just passing by. I delivered a baby the other side of Lyon Creek this morning." He began to unwind the bandage. The strips of cloth were dirty where Quint had hobbled about the house and yard.

"You been putting weight on this foot?" Doc asked.

"Some," Quint said. "Had to. I used this, though." He showed Doc the crutch Maud had made. She had searched the creek bank for a sapling that branched into a wide V, had cut the green wood to Quint's length and padded the V to fit under his arm.

Doc said, "Gosh sakes, you are fixed up! Pays to have females to take care of you. But stay off that leg as much as you can for another three weeks."

Quint looked dissatisfied. "Have you seen my brother?" he asked.

Doc shook his head.

"I thought he'd ride out."

"He's probably still herding cattle," Doc said. "The railroad can't handle all the cattle waiting to be shipped."

Over supper Doc told them more news. Indians had stampeded a trail herd. A band of no-count white men—discharged soldiers, some people said—were ranging the prairie, stealing and murdering. Cholera had cropped up in town and elsewhere. Two cowboys had died of it on the trail. The waiting herds had eaten all the grass for miles around town. Cattle running loose in Abilene had cleaned out the gardens. A woman or child hardly dared step outside for fear of meeting a half-wild steer. The number of saloons and dance halls had doubled.

Maud watched Quint. All this talk about goings-on in town made her wish to go. She guessed he felt the same, but there was no reason to make a trip. The hot weather was keeping even the Coddingtons at home. It was the middle of August. The hot dry wind might go on blowing for several weeks yet.

Before breakfast the following Sunday, a group of men rode into the yard. They were clean-shaven, their clothes new and unfaded. One man swung down from his horse and came toward the door. He removed his hat and said, "Howdy, ma'am" before Maud recognized him as the dirty, bearded trail boss of Quint's outfit. But Quint came from the outhouse at a limping run.

"Where's Verne?" he shouted with a laugh. "Throwed in jail?"

Belle came to the doorway. The trail boss shook his head. "It's real bad news, son. Verne stopped a bullet Friday night."

Belle and Maud gasped. Quint's face lost its color. His mouth went awry.

"He never knew what hit him," the boss said. "I'm sorry to be the one to tell you, boy."

"Oh, Quint," Belle said. "I'm so sorry!" She laid a hand on his arm.

He pulled away and turned his back. His shoulders began to shake. "Oh, hell!" he choked and stumbled away around the corner of the house.

"Let him go," the boss said. "You can tell him later how it happened. There was some gunplay, and Verne happened to be on the sidelines. He got a bullet through the neck. Never knew what hit him."

"Poor Quint," Belle whispered. "He admired his brother so. The doctor says it'll be another month before he can ride—"

The trail boss spat tobacco, wiped his chin, and looked embarrassed. "I got more men than I need now. And no cows, see?"

"But—"

"Verne was a good man. You tell the boy I said that. We brought his saddle and his gun. Henry—" One of the men dismounted and carried a saddle to the lean-to. Atop it he laid a holstered pistol.

"My goodness, I hope that's not loaded," Belle said.

"No, ma'am." The foreman pulled a brown envelope from his pocket. "Here's Quint's pay, and what Verne had left. Tell Quint we buried Verne decent.

Took up a collection. Ladies, we got a long ride—" He mounted his horse, raised his hat, and gathered the reins. The other men raised their hats, too.

The group set off at an easy trot that would carry them over the miles. Maud and Belle watched them disappear into a draw and reappear on the other side, smaller, blurred by heat waves.

"Should I go find Quint?" Maud broke the silence.

Belle sighed. "Give him a little time. You can take him a cup of coffee when it's ready."

· 9 ·
Toughing It Out

MAUD FOUND QUINT behind the house, his back against the wall. He was staring across the prairie with red-rimmed eyes.

"Coffee?" Maud offered the cup.

He took it without looking at her.

She said, "Do you want to hear what happened?"

He shrugged, as though the details didn't matter. Maud told him while he sipped his coffee. She wondered if she should keep him company for a while, but the chickens needed to be let out. Belle was in the shed milking Lady, and then it would be Maud's chore to take her to pasture.

They got through the day somehow. Maud and Belle only spoke when necessary, allowing their sober faces to express their sympathy.

Once Quint said, "I keep forgetting he's dead, and

then remembering again. I wish I could have been there. I don't even know where he's buried."

"The ceremony helps," Belle agreed.

What would Quint do now? Maud wished he could stay on with them, but he had his living to earn. She hoped he wouldn't go back to Texas. If he found a job in Abilene, he might ride out to visit sometimes. As the days passed, his sorrow eased, but the question of his future remained.

One evening toward the end of August, the heat and drought was broken by a fierce rainstorm. Lightning crackled, thunder rolled, and hailstones pounded down on the dusty earth, and battered the roof. Rivulets of muddy water found ways through the dry, cracked sod and poured down upon rug and beds. Poor Spot was terrified by the storm. He whined and shivered and begged to come inside. When they let him in, he crept under Quint's bed.

When it was over, they turned in, hoping the roof wouldn't spring new leaks while they slept.

They awoke to a cool, cloudy morning.

"This is the day to see Mr. Randolph," Belle announced. "We'll take the wagon. Quint can come, too."

Maud took Lady to pasture and set out to catch Sam. He'd been free so long she expected him to be troublesome, but perhaps like herself, he welcomed a change. At any rate, he didn't kick up his heels until he was bridled and she was riding him bareback to the house. Then he broke into a gallop and would have gone right on down the track, but Maud clung to his mane, shouting and screaming, until he turned into the yard.

Harnessing him to the wagon, she caught herself whistling. She glanced over her shoulder to see if anyone had heard. Whistling was most unladylike, but she hadn't been farther from home than Charlie Haynes's place for weeks.

Belle came out wearing her corsets and good black dress. Maud brought the wagon to the door so Quint wouldn't have to walk far. They settled him on a quilt in the wagon bed where he could keep his leg straight.

Maud drove slowly, to keep from jolting him, but also to make the trip last longer.

Mr. Randolph's place lay a mile the other side of Dry Creek, but with the wagon they had to go by the ford, which meant going round past Shorty's and Charlie's places.

When Belle saw the muddy rush of water pouring over the ford, she shrieked at Maud to take care. Maud knew the water wasn't deep and drove fearlessly through. The water barely touched the axles. At the top of the other bank, she turned left and drove across the prairie.

Mr. Randolph had built his house before the war. A row of half-grown cedar trees protected barn and house from the north wind. He was a widower. A woman named Mrs. Jones cooked for him and kept his house clean.

They found him ready to ride to town. However, he got down from his horse and took Belle away to what he called his study. Maud and Quint waited in the kitchen. Mrs. Jones gave them fresh-baked bread and buttermilk and tried to learn the reason for Belle's visit.

After no more than five minutes Belle came back looking unhappy. Mr. Randolph didn't look pleased to see Maud and Quint either. He bowed himself out of the door, and they heard him ride off. Belle's eyes were pink round the rims. She looked as though she wanted to cry. As soon as they could escape Mrs. Jones's eager chitchat, Maud clucked to Sam and they drove away.

"There isn't going to be any school!" Belle spoke above the rattle of the wagon.

"How can that be?" Maud cried.

Belle shrugged. "He says the grasshoppers have driven out all the families. I told him the Martins are still here, and Mr. Haynes's youngsters, and you, Maud. I even said Quint would be going to school, but it didn't help. He's convinced we'll all have to leave before winter. I believe he's glad. He wants this to be cattle country."

"What if everyone's still here?" Maud demanded.

Belle shook her head without answering.

Something cold clutched at Maud's innards. She had been so sure that if Belle began teaching school, she would feel a part of the community by the end of the year. Besides that, she would be earning money and wouldn't have to spend what she'd brought with her. Now they were going to have to buy corn, and with no money coming in. . . . Maud felt close to tears, too. Grimly she made up her mind to snare all the rabbits and prairie chickens she could, but she knew from experience that days could go by when you didn't catch anything, just when you were the hungriest for a taste of fresh meat.

They drove the rest of the way in gloomy silence.

Maud pulled up in front of the door. Belle climbed stiffly down. Together they helped Quint out.

"School or no school, I'm not giving up now," Belle said. "We'll make what we have stretch. That's all."

"We'll tough it out," Maud agreed, but her heart felt like a chunk of sod. Belle might tough it out for the winter, but by spring she'd have had enough. Maud was tempted to shrug off such cares for the future. It was hard to look that far ahead, but Mr. Nelson had once told her that an orphan must plan her own life.

The best thing she could do, Maud decided, was to learn all she could from Belle while she had the chance; and maybe, by being cheerful and helpful, she could make Belle like their home so much she wouldn't want to leave, even if they didn't have a lot to eat.

"WHEN WAS SCHOOL supposed to start?" Quint asked. He was stretched on his bed looking tired.

"October or November," Belle told him. "The district has enough money for a five-month school—if they have any pupils."

Quint studied the calendar. "My leg will be healed in a week or so."

"Not healed!" Belle exclaimed. "That's when Doctor Owen said you could take the splints off. You'll have to take care for some weeks after that."

Quint sighed. "By that time all the winter jobs will be taken—if there are any."

"Quint, what would you think of staying here through the winter and helping us?"

"What kind of help could I be, except to eat your food?"

"I'm sure your being here has kept the Coddingtons from pestering us," Belle said.

Maud held her breath. Quint was sweet on Belle. Was it enough to keep him here? Maud wanted him to stay, even though it meant another mouth to feed. She wasn't sure why, but everything seemed more exciting with him around.

She said, "The Coddingtons aren't the only ones. As soon as the weather cools off, all the single men around here will come courting."

"Oh, I hope not!" Belle blushed.

"I don't want to be a burden," Quint said stubbornly.

"We need someone who knows how to load a gun and shoot it," Belle said.

Quint's eyes brightened. Then he hid the expression with a scowl. "You're welcome to the money I've got."

Belle shook her head. "Quint, that's good of you, but—"

"No, it ain't. If I'd been in town at a boarding house, it would've been gone by now. Except I've got to have some new britches. These look like I stole my little brother's."

They did. They showed three inches of bare ankle, and the patches on the seat had been repatched. Silas's trousers were too short for Quint, too.

"Let's see what happens," Belle said. "When it's

time for your splints to come off, we'll take a trip to town." She disappeared behind the curtain to change her dress.

Sam was waiting to be unhitched. With confused feelings Maud went out to do it. It looked as if Quint was going to stay. That was wonderful. And they had a cow. But not to have any school. . . . Her heart sank. How the winter would drag!

The weather grew hot again. The tireless wind blew. However, the days were growing shorter, the shadows growing longer. The heat couldn't last forever.

THE NEXT TIME Shorty Haynes drove up, Maud feared he had come to tell them he was leaving. Instead he declared that nothing or nobody was going to make him give up his claim. "I aim to win my bet," he said, whiskers bristling.

"What bet?" Belle asked.

"Why, my bet with Uncle Sam! He's betting me ten dollars to a hundred and sixty acres that I can't hold out here for five years. I aim to win."

"Good for you, Mr. Haynes," Belle said. "May I tell Mr. Randolph that?"

"I'll tell him myself, first time I see him. I'm on the school board, too, you know. He's got no right to close the school without consulting me."

"WE'LL HAVE TO WAIT," Belle told Quint and Maud when Shorty had gone. "If the Martins are still here by the end of September, I'll call on Mr. Randolph again. Surely the Martins won't leave. Where would they go?"

Early in September, on the day Quint had figured the splints could come off, he removed them as soon as he woke up. A thunderstorm the night before had cooled the air. It was barely daylight when Maud and Belle came from behind their curtain. Quint was balanced gingerly on both feet.

"My leg sure feels funny," he said by way of greeting. He clutched the corner of the table for support. "I don't seem to have any strength in my knee," he complained.

"Please don't walk around too much before you see the doctor," Belle begged.

At breakfast the sound of a horse's hooves made them look at each other. Maud was first to reach the door.

"It's Charlie Dexter."

"He wants to see how Miss Belle looks early in the morning," Quint said. Now that he felt at home, he was becoming a tease.

Charlie, however, had something else on his mind. "I come to say goodbye," he told them shyly. "I'm going back to Iowa."

"Not for good!" Maud cried.

Charlie shook his head. "For the winter. I'm going back to my folks' farm. If I can't find work, at least they'll feed me."

"What if somebody moves into your house?" Maud worried.

Charlie shrugged. "Have to chance that. If I starve to death, they'll move in anyway."

Belle offered him coffee and cornbread crumbled in milk. There was sugar for the coffee if he wished.

"Much obliged." Charlie grew red in the face. "All I've had lately is cornmeal mush."

"Quint took his splints off this morning so we're celebrating," Belle explained. "We're going to town. We planned to drive around by your place and Mr. Haynes's to see if you needed anything."

"Is Shorty looking after your geese?" Maud asked.

Charlie looked embarrassed. "I ate them."

Belle offered to lend him two dollars for the road, but he shook his head, blushing again. "I ain't borrowed from a lady yet. I'll get along."

There was a small hunk of bacon left. She pressed that on him and wrapped the remains of the cornbread in one of Silas's handkerchiefs.

When he had gone, Quint said, "You gave away the cornbread, Miss Belle. What are we going to eat for dinner?"

"We'll have dinner in Abilene," Belle said grandly. "We need something to make us feel prosperous."

Maud had put Sam in the stable the night before so she wouldn't have to chase him up and down the creek. Quint harnessed him while Maud hauled from the well the butter they meant to sell in town.

Despite saying goodbye to Charlie, they set out in good spirits, Maud driving. The sun had scarcely risen above the horizon.

They did indeed spend a grand day in town. They drove first to Doc's office. He was out. At the post office Belle received a letter from her brother and picked up one for Shorty. Then it was nearly noon and they were hungry. So they tied Sam to a hitching rail and crossed the street to the hotel.

Dinner there consisted of much the same food as they ate at home, but it was a treat to eat off strange crockery in the company of other diners. Quint insisted on paying the bill.

As they were leaving the dining room, Doc Owen walked in. He took Quint into the empty parlor to look at his leg. Belle and Maud waited on the hotel porch.

"Look at that!" Belle exclaimed.

A covered wagon was rolling along the dusty street, a woman and a child on the seat beside the driver. Painted on the side of the canvas was the wry message: "Going East to visit my wife's relations."

When the wagon had gone on down the street, Belle said, "I heard at the post office that the Government is shipping in corn. At least it will be available for money. I think I'll buy what I can."

The doctor and Quint joined them on the porch.

"Looks okay to me," the doctor said, "But if it starts to hurt, he's to get off it."

Quint left to buy his new clothes. His boots hid his bare ankles, but no one could deny that Silas Nelson's old shirt and vest didn't fit too well.

Wrapped in wet sacks under the wagon seat, the butter was still cool. The storekeeper took it in trade. It paid for a small part of the supplies they needed. Belle's list was long; there was no telling when they would get to town again, if the weather turned bad.

Maud still had some of the money Mr. Nelson had paid her. With it she bought material to make Quint a shirt for Christmas, and she bought yarn to knit a muffler for Belle. A muffler wasn't very stylish, but it was something she knew how to make, and Belle might be glad to have it when winter came. She paid the storekeeper's wife for her purchases and tucked them out of sight in the wagon. She intended to give the rest of her money to Belle to use for all of them.

A minute later Quint came along in his new blue jeans, a store-bought shirt, and a new vest. He had had his boots shined and his hat cleaned, and he looked so grown-up Maud was tongue-tied. At least she didn't feel shabby. She was wearing one of the new dresses Belle had helped her make, and her best sunbonnet.

Belle arrived soon after with her arms full, and the storekeeper followed, carrying the kerosene can and the bag of oats for Sam.

Quint jumped down to help, forgetting his leg, and grunted with pain.

"Oh, Quint, do be careful!" Belle scolded. Then once all the purchases were stowed away, she complimented Quint on his new elegance.

He bowed. "Would you ladies like to have some refreshments before we leave?"

Belle laughed. "It seems a shame not to let you take us somewhere to show off your clothes."

They found the hotel dining room closed till suppertime. Since no lady could go into a saloon, Quint had to be content with strolling down the street with Belle and Maud on either arm. By the time they returned to the wagon, he was limping. He dropped onto the seat with a sigh.

It was time to go home.

NEXT DAY SHORTY HAYNES came to tell them he'd met
the Coddingtons while he was out hunting. Jake Coddington told him they were leaving for the winter.

Belle's eyes brightened, and Maud felt a great sense
of relief. True, the Coddingtons hadn't bothered them,
but you never knew when they might get drunk and
decide to make good their threats.

SEPTEMBER PASSED and October came. Still they heard
nothing about opening the school.

"I can't go begging Mr. Randolph again," Belle
said. "It's up to Shorty—I mean, Mr. Haynes—to settle
it."

The year before Maud and her sister had gathered
wild plums and dried them. This year there were none.
The grasshoppers had eaten them.

On their way south, geese and ducks stopped overnight on the creek. Quint got a goose with a lucky shot
from his brother's revolver. The prairie chickens Maud
snared were fat from all the grasshoppers they had
eaten, but their flesh seemed to taste grasshoppery.

THEN ONE SATURDAY near the end of October Shorty
and his two youngsters made the trip to Abilene. Early
darkness was approaching when they stopped off to deliver a letter from Belle's brother. Belle invited them in.

"Don't mind if I do," Shorty said. "We're in no hurry to get home. The moon's like daylight these nights."

Belle invited them to share the supper she had cooked. She hadn't needed much practice to learn to stir up cornbread and bake squash. They were saving the flour for special occasions.

"Bud, Luanne, wash your hands," Shorty ordered. He sat on the corner of the bed. Belle returned to her mending. She was sitting in the chair Shorty had made for her.

"Now that sure is a pretty sight!" he said and sighed.

Quint met Maud's eye and winked, but Maud wasn't amused. She found she was holding her breath. What awkward thing would Shorty say next? However, he went on to talk about what he'd done in Abilene.

After supper he accepted a second cup of coffee and leaned his forearms on the table. "I've been thinking," he said. "I've come to the conclusion that two women hadn't ought to spend the winter alone. If we was to get a three-day blizzard, I wouldn't be able to get over here, much as I'd like to. No, sir, I don't believe two women can survive alone."

Maud looked round the room, her indignation rising. Everything looked so snug! The rug and floor were swept. Quint's bed was covered with one of Belle's patchwork quilts. Their clothes were clean and mended.

By contrast Luanne and Bud might have been dressed from the ragbag. Luanne's hair needed rebraiding, and she kept scratching. Lice, most likely. Maud had been inside Shorty's house. It was a mess!

Belle, too, was looking thoughtfully at Luanne. Shorty sensed the direction of her thoughts.

"Luanne needs a woman's touch," he said.

Belle said, "Not having lived through a winter here, I'm no expert. But I believe we're ready for it."

"Well—" Shorty fidgeted. He was finding it hard to promote his cause. "I see you've got your cowchips stacked."

"Yes." Belle finished taking the dishes off the table. "What about the school?" she asked. "Mr. Martin was here after you left. He's going to Kansas City to look for work. His wife and the children are staying. Have you spoken to Mr. Randolph?"

Shorty shook his head. "I drove over, but he'd gone off someplace. We ought to call on him together. I'll tell him we need the school and we need you to teach it."

"All right," Belle agreed.

Shorty looked pleased until Belle added, "We'll take Maud and your children as a reminder." Then he looked put out. He must have been hoping to have a drive alone with Belle. Maud laughed to herself.

"I wisht I could get me a job," Shorty rambled on. "There's nothing to do on a claim now but sit back and wait for spring. You used to that kind of life?"

Belle smiled. "A woman can do nothing as well as a man, Mr. Haynes."

Shorty wasn't ready to give up. He turned to Quint. "Your leg mending pretty well? I supose you'll be leaving soon."

"Miss Belle's asked me to stay." Quint's voice was smug.

"Oh! In that case—" Shorty flushed and got to his feet. "You won't need my protection."

"We'll have the protection of Providence, which is all anyone can hope for," Belle said.

"Then you won't be upset to learn you've got a new neighbor," Shorty growled. "I wasn't going to tell you 'cause I didn't want to scare you. Somebody's moved into Coddington's dugout. He's wearing a gun and looking mighty unfriendly. Wouldn't surprise me if he turned out to be a claim jumper." Shorty stalked to the door. "Kids! Time you was in bed."

It would have been impolite not to follow the Hayneses out to their wagon. Quint tossed Luanne up onto the seat beside her brother.

"The sooner we call on Mr. Randolph, the better," Belle said.

"I suppose so," Shorty growled. He slapped his horses with the reins and drove off.

"I'm afraid I made him angry," Belle said as they turned back to the house.

"Couldn't be helped," Quint replied.

The full moon cast sharp shadows. Maud lingered outside, trying to put a name to the uneasy feeling the moonlight gave her. Up by the empty schoolhouse a coyote began to yip. From the other side of Dry Creek another barked in reply. For a moment Maud imagined herself a coyote, running wild across the prairie or singing to the moon.

From the stable came a rustling sound. Lady and her calf were settling themselves for the night. Spot came trotting back from having seen the wagon on its way. Maud shivered. Tomorrow morning the prairie would be white with frost. Alluring as the moonlight was, her heart swelled at the thought of the warm room where she belonged and the two people there. She hoped, oh she yearned for the life she was now living to go on and on. Nothing had ever been so good. But what could she do to keep it?

Belle and Quint were discussing the new neighbor.

"He must be a friend of the Coddingtons," Belle was saying. "That doesn't necessarily mean he's disreputable."

"Only probably." Quint laughed. "It's a strange time of year to move onto a claim."

"Maybe he's hiding out," Maud said brightly. She wasn't afraid. Nobody could be as bad as the Coddingtons.

"Mercy, don't say that!" Belle cried. "Promise me, both of you, that until we know more about him you'll keep out of his way."

Shorty wasn't a man to stay mad. He turned up two mornings later, with Bud and Luanne. Luanne's hair was freshly braided. Bud's hair had been cut—or rather, chopped.

"Ready to go see Randolph?" Shorty called.

Belle invited them in to wait while she put on her good dress. When they set out, she rode beside Shorty. With the rest of them in back, they made quite a wagonload.

"That's some family you've got there!" Mr. Randolph teased Shorty when they drove into his yard. He seemed to have already made up his mind about the school because he said, "You've made your point. I hear Martins are still here, too. When do you want to start?"

Both men looked at Belle.

"The second week in November," Belle said firmly.

Maud didn't say anything, but she found herself grinning crazily at Bud, who grinned happily back.

"What made you choose that date, Miss Belle?" Quint asked when they were back home and Shorty had gone.

Belle looked mischievous. "I didn't want to seem too anxious."

Maud gave a sigh of contentment. "Now we don't have a thing to worry about."

"Just the outlaw next door." Quint rolled his eyes and tried to look scared.

"Please!" Belle shivered.

Maud and Quint helped clean the schoolhouse. They dusted benches and washed the windows and swept up dead wasps and last year's tracked-in mud. Quint cut the weeds in the schoolyard.

On the Monday morning school was to start, they found the other pupils waiting for them, including the five Martin children. Eulalia, the eldest, was the only girl in school close to Maud's age. They hadn't seen each other all summer. Eliza, the youngest Martin child, and Luanne Haynes were starting first grade. Early in the spring a new family had built a soddy a mile south of the schoolhouse. They had a boy, Henry, who was Bud's age. They, too, had decided to tough it out.

Belle called everyone in, assigned seats, and the term began. Everyone was excited to be there. It was a change from the long, boring summer.

THE WEATHER STAYED WARM. Maud and Quint had plenty to do after school. Days were so short they barely had time to get the chores done before dark. Sam had to be brought in at night now in case the weather turned bad. They taught him to come of his own accord by feeding him a handful of oats each evening. The calf now grazed alongside his mother.

Maud took charge of the milk, setting the cream to rise and making butter. Lady was no pedigreed Jersey. They easily used up the amount of milk she gave, one way and another.

Maud showed Quint how to snare rabbits and prairie chickens. He looked down his nose at this way of securing meat until he tried hunting them with the revolver and returned disgruntled and empty-handed.

"You ladies don't need me at all! If I left you this gun and taught you to load it, I'd never be missed."

"Of course you'd be missed," Belle soothed him. "Who'd split the wood and build the fires?"

"Maud would," he said, but he grinned.

Maud wanted to say, "We like having you around," but just thinking the words made her heart beat harder. She couldn't imagine saying them aloud.

LATE ONE CLOUDY AFTERNOON Maud knelt in the tall grass setting a snare. She had discovered a new rabbit run not far from Jake Coddington's boundary. From where she knelt, she felt rather than heard hoofbeats and sat back on her heels to see who was riding along the track.

She'd never seen the horse before. It was black, with a white star on its forehead. The rider was wearing a black hat and an old gray overcoat—not an army coat, though he rode like a soldier. A black beard covered the lower part of his face. He didn't seem to see her crouched in the grass, but she couldn't be sure. The wide-brimmed hat hid his eyes. A sack of grain lay across the horse's rump. A bulky bag hung from the saddle. This was the man living in Jake's dugout!

Sure enough, he turned downhill toward the creek. Between the pale grass and the heavy sky the black horse and the rider stood out like a picture in a book.

A shiver ran over Maud. Somehow she knew he was different from Shorty Haynes and Charlie Dexter. And for some reason, when she returned to the house, she didn't mention seeing him.

A WEEK LATER, walking home from school, they all saw him. Again he was coming from town, his horse laden with a canvas-wrapped bundle. He lifted his hat, but passed them without speaking.

"Did you see that coat?" Quint muttered. "That's a Confederate coat!"

Maud said, "Then he can't be a friend of the Coddingtons. Jake still brags about killing Rebels."

"An army coat doesn't make a man a soldier," Quint said. "Look at me." He was wearing Silas Nelson's blue army coat. "I wonder how he came by that horse."

"The less we know about him, the better," Belle said. "Mind your business and let's enjoy our peace."

· 10 ·
The
Squatter

THE FIRST SATURDAY in December was warm and sunny.
Belle and Maud were taking advantage of the mild
weather to turn the house inside out. First they put the
chairs and table outside so Belle could sweep the hard-
packed dirt floor. They hung the carpet over the meat-
drying rack. Maud was trying to beat some of the dust
out of it when she caught sight of a horse and rider
approaching. When she saw who it was, her heart
seemed to catch in her throat. Jake Coddington!

And Quint had disappeared when the housecleaning began.

Jake dismounted without being invited. He seemed
to have come for a visit. He accepted a cup of buttermilk and sat in the willow chair. There was nothing for
it but to stop work and sit down, too. The dust had to

settle, anyhow, before they could replace the furniture and bedding.

After a bit of chitchat about the weather, Jake suddenly said, "I hear there's a damned Rebel holed up in my dugout."

Maud's heart thudded.

Belle looked frightened, too. After a moment she said, "Maud and Quint and I are at school all day. I'm teaching, you know."

"You ain't seen him, then?"

Belle shrugged. "Mr. Haynes told us he'd seen someone. We thought he must be a friend of yours."

"No, he sure ain't!" Jake spat tobacco juice and wiped his beard. "He's a danged Rebel, and a card sharp, and I don't know what-all. Some folks say he ain't even a Rebel, that he deserted Uncle Sam's army. All I know is, I'm going to drive him off my claim." He took a bottle of whisky from his coat pocket and pulled out the cork. "You ladies don't mind if I perk up this buttermilk, do you?"

Not waiting for an answer, he poured a lot of whisky into the milk and asked Maud for a spoon. She brought it, he stirred the concoction and drank it off. Then he wiped his beard. "Good buttermilk!" he said. "I wouldn't mind another cupful, if you could spare it."

Maud went to get it. She wished Quint would return. Everyone said that the more Jake Coddington drank, the meaner he got.

"Don't you worry, ma'am," he was telling Belle. "I aim to run that jumper clean out of the country." He patted the gun on his hip. "He been bothering anybody?"

"Not that I know of. How did you hear about this man?"

"Hear about him? Oh—" Jake waved a hand. "Someone in town told me."

"Abilene?"

Jake poured whiskey into the second cup of buttermilk. He swallowed half and smacked his lips. "That's right. Why work when I can make money gambling?" He laughed with smug satisfaction.

"What is Eph doing?" Belle asked.

"He went to Missouri. Supposed to be working. I'm through paying his keep. Say, is it true that Rebel cuss wears a gun?"

Belle looked haughty. "I couldn't tell you. I haven't seen him."

"Shorty says he does," Maud told Jake with satisfaction. Because she was afraid of Jake Coddington, she was ready to side with anyone he was against.

Jake drained his cup and got to his feet. "I reckon I'll pay him a visit."

Maud felt a great sense of relief. Apparently Jake Coddington hadn't come to make trouble for Belle. Nevertheless, Maud just plain couldn't stand him. He was mean, and he was a bully, and probably worse things she didn't know about.

Before remounting, Jake took a long swig from his bottle. Working up courage, Maud thought. She hoped the stranger was tougher and meaner than Jake.

The two young women set about putting the house back together. They had carried in the furniture and were stuffing fresh hay into the mattresses when they heard shots. The shots came from the direction of Jake's claim. They stared at each other.

"He hasn't had time to get there," Belle said.

"I guess he has," Maud said. "Unless it's Quint shooting rabbits."

"I wish Quint would come back," Belle fretted. "If there's going to be trouble, I want to know where he is."

"Maybe they've shot each other," Maud suggested.

"Who?" Belle gasped.

"Jake Coddington and the deserter."

Belle shut her eyes. "Don't say that!"

Maud bit her lip. "Deserter?"

"No! I meant, please don't suggest they may have killed each other. But you shouldn't call someone a deserter unless you know. Not even then. Ladies shouldn't know about such people."

"How can we help knowing? He's our nearest neighbor."

Belle returned to her dusting. "I don't know— Back East nice people didn't have such neighbors."

"Out here, there's no Sunday west of Junction City," Maud quoted.

"You know that isn't true," Belle scolded. "Abilene has three churches."

And twenty saloons, Maud was about to add when the sound of a horse galloping made her spring to the door.

The horse pounded into the yard, riderless, stirrups flapping.

"Jake's!" Maud screeched.

The animal stopped at the stable and put his head

inside. Spot circled him, stiff-legged. The horse took fright and wheeled. It galloped around the corner of the stable, and Maud heard it pounding on in the general direction of the creek.

Round-eyed Belle stared at her. "What do we do now?"

Maud took off her apron. "I'll see if I can catch it."

"Not the horse!" Belle laughed shakily. "Jake!"

Maud said thoughtfully, "I guess it wouldn't hurt to walk that way. The other fellow's got no call to shoot us. Not as long as we stay on our land."

They hadn't gone far when they saw Jake limping toward them.

Belle halted. "That one's still alive," she whispered.

Maud stopped, too. "Darn!" she muttered.

"Maud!" Belle sounded shocked. "You didn't want him shot, did you? You shouldn't wish anyone ill-luck."

Maud made a face. She said, "I was hoping the other fellow would drive him away."

Jake drew near, his face red, his eyes angry. One side of his coat was wet. Blood! Then Maud's nose caught the smell of whisky. "He's broken his bottle." A giggle burst from her.

"Are you hurt?" Belle asked when Jake came up to them.

He had trouble telling them. "That—, that—" His eyes bulged. He couldn't swear before ladies, and he was too angry to think of other words.

"That son-of-a-gun Rebel varmint!" he managed at last. "He shot at me! Then he barricaded himself into *my* dugout. If my gol—, I mean gosh-durned horse hadn't threw me, I'd have smoked the—, the sucker out of there. I'd have nailed his hide to the door! Did you see him?" Jake meant his horse.

Maud said, "He came running into the yard. That's what brought us out. He's probably in the pasture with Sam by now."

"I think my ankle's sprained," Jake whined.

"Then you ought to get your boot off," Belle said. "I'll give you one of Mr. Nelson's socks to wear back to town."

Maud felt a mad desire to laugh. What if they had Jake on their hands, too?

"If you want to wait here, I'll catch your horse," Maud offered.

"I can limp to the house," Jake said. "You got anything to drink?"

"Buttermilk . . . water," Belle said.

"Naw, I meant booze!"

"Certainly not," Belle said.

" 'Course not," Jake muttered glumly. He limped in one wheel track, Belle walked in the other, Maud brought up the rear.

At the house, Belle built up the fire and made coffee. The afternoon was growing colder. Maud put her shawl over her shoulders, crossed the ends across her chest, and tied them behind her back. Then she set out to find Jake's horse, willing to give any aid that would set the man on his way.

Expecting trouble, she took along a handful of oats to lure Sam. Sure enough, Jake's horse was nearby, cropping grass. Maud whistled. At sight of her outstretched hand Sam came willingly, and she climbed on his back. Jake's horse sidled nervously and looked ready to run, but he let Sam approach. Maud grabbed the trailing reins. Triumphantly she led him to the house.

Jake limped out, one foot padded with rags, carrying his boot in his hand. He would have used it to give his horse a beating if Maud had not screamed and threatened to let the animal go again.

Scowling, Jake climbed into the saddle. Without a word he kicked his heels into the creature's flanks and set off at a trot.

"Good riddance to bad rubbish," Belle said. They watched Jake ride away. "You didn't see Quint, did you?"

"No."

Belle frowned. "He shouldn't go off without telling us. Jake said the other man began shooting as soon as he saw him. One of the shots creased the horse's flank. That's why Jake got thrown. The claim jumper ran inside and barred the door. Jake claims he didn't do any shooting at all. Do you suppose he's telling the truth?"

"Probably not," Maud said.

"He was full of what he'll do when he comes back. I wish Quint were here. Who knows what he did to that man."

"Want me to go and look?" Maud asked. "I mean, I can see if he's walking around."

"I don't want him to think we're snooping. Good gracious, where can Quint be? I hope he hasn't managed to get himself lost."

"He couldn't," Maud said.

Belle shook her head. "I don't know how you and Quint manage not to. Everywhere in this country looks the same."

It doesn't! Maud wanted to say, but one mustn't contradict grownups. "You'd let Quint go, but not me," she stated.

"Ladies don't call on bachelors."

"I didn't mean *call* on him," Maud protested. "I could walk over and take a look without his seeing me."

"Can you?"

"Sure. I can peek over the bank, and he'll never know."

"Are you sure?"

"Yes."

Belle straightened her shoulders. "We'll both go! It's an errand of mercy, after all."

Putting on shawls, they called Spot and set out across the prairie. Spot was happy to be going anywhere.

At the rim of the bank Maud crept forward, knelt, and peered through the long grass. Smoke was coming from the dugout, but nobody was to be seen. She beckoned to Belle. Together they peered across the creek. A smaller dugout served as a stable. When the Coddingtons lived there, the latter was always half hidden by a big pile of manure. Now the manure pile was gone. The dooryard was neater than Maud had ever seen it.

"I guess Jake was telling the truth," Maud said.

"The fire would go on burning, no matter what," Belle whispered.

They crouched in the grass, wondering what to do. And while they watched, the door opened. A man came out carrying a bucket, who was, of course, the stranger. He looked up and down the creek, then strolled to the water and waited while the bucket filled. Maud and Belle made themselves as small as possible. He carried the water inside and shut the door.

Hampered by skirts, Maud and Belle crawled backwards till they could stand up without being seen.

"I'm satisfied," Belle said. "Let's go home. If Quint's back, he'll wonder where we are."

"Tit for tat," Maud said.

Belle smiled. "I'm sure we've had a more exciting day."

Maud was quiet during the walk. She wanted to like the squatter. Any enemy of Jake's was a friend of hers. But that didn't mean this man could be trusted, either.

"A man who can scare Jake Coddington must be real bad," she said at last.

"I was thinking the same," Belle agreed. "I'm glad we have Quint. If you and I were alone, I wouldn't be able to sleep at night."

"He looked *clean*," Maud ventured.

"That's mysterious in itself," Belle said. "How can a man living in a dirty cave in the ground keep his clothes clean?"

Quint was home, with nothing to show for his day's hunting. All he had to tell was that he had stopped at Kackley's to talk to George and Iva. They had asked after Maud, but still hadn't forgiven her for choosing to live with Belle.

JAKE's VISIT provided conversation for days. Though Christmas was approaching, the weather stayed good, and twice they saw the squatter ride past, coming back from Abilene. Each time he had a sackful of supplies tied to his saddle.

"What do you suppose he's carrying?" Quint asked the second time the man passed. "He must eat more than anybody in the country."

"Stocking up," Maud offered.

The fact that the man risked traveling back and forth so often gave rise to other curiosity. Didn't he know a blizzard could whirl out of the north, blotting out landmarks in minutes?

The squatter's foolhardiness made Shorty decide to take a chance, too. Christmas was near; the weather continued warm; the moon was again full. He went to town one school day. He stopped to tell Belle he was going and would do her errands. Bud and Luanne were to walk home with Maud and await their father there.

"He'll get back just in time for supper," Maud predicted.

Sure enough, at the end of the day six people crowded round the supper table. Luanne and Bud liked Maud's cooking much better than their father's, but that wasn't saying much, Maud reflected.

Yet they all welcomed the gossip Shorty brought.

Squeezed into the small room, they listened eagerly. Much of it pertained to new buildings going up in town. "You know that corner with the young cottonwoods? That's going to be another dance hall."

Not till the meal was over did he mention the most interesting item.

"Say, I met Doc Owen headed out to Big Creek. He asked how we was getting along with our new neighbor."

"Does he know him?" Maud asked.

Shorty shook his head. "He heard he was a friend of Jake Coddington's till they fell out. I said we didn't know his name, and we weren't certain we wanted to. Doc said Postmaster told him the man came in to pick up a package. The paper was pretty well torn, and when Postmaster handed it to him—'Southern' Doc called him, or maybe 'the Southerner'—anyhow, the package come apart. What do you suppose was in it?"

Quint guessed pistols; Belle guessed seeds; Maud picked the most unlikely thing she could think of: "Bibles."

Shorty grinned. "You guessed close, young lady. Postmaster said it was books."

"Really?" Maud squeaked. "What do you suppose . . . ?" Her voice trailed off.

"A book salesman," Quint chortled. "Not an outlaw at all!"

Shorty took his children home soon after, leaving his neighbors with a lively topic of discussion. Was the man's name Southern, or had Doc called him the Southerner? Either sounded better than calling him the squatter, a name that wasn't too safe to say out loud.

A Christmas celebration was planned to be held at the schoolhouse. Everyone was to be invited, of course, whether they had children in school or not.

"What about Mr. Southern?" Maud asked. Since Shorty's report about the books, Maud was more curious than ever. Did the man really have books—books that could be borrowed if only they knew him? Neither Belle nor Quint put faith in the story. Oh, he might have received a magazine or two; but a package of books? Unlikely. Maud knew the postmaster was a great gossip. Belle said it was more likely the man was an outlaw and Maud was to stay far away from that side of the claim.

As the other members of the Christmas committee, Shorty Haynes and Wes Randolph came to the sod house on a Sunday to discuss the party. Belle mentioned the man in Coddington's dugout. Should he be invited? Someone must decide.

"He's not part of the community," Shorty said.

Wes Randolph agreed. "I heard about him in town last week. He calls himself Tom Southern. He was run out of Texas and came to Abilene with a partner. They weren't there more than a few days when his partner run off. There was shooting."

"Bad men, us Texans," Quint murmured, making Maud giggle. He and she were sitting on the end of the bed to be out of the way while the committee sat round the table. Maud was practicing crochet stitches with string.

"Are you sure it's the same man?" Belle asked.

"Why wouldn't it be?" Wes Randolph's voice grew loud, as though Belle questioned his word. "He's an army deserter—not from Uncle Sam's army, you may be sure! But a man that gets drove out of Texas has got to be a rough customer. He's hiding out! Jake Coddington probably told him he could stay here, and then they had a falling out. If he does any farming, I'll eat my hat! That horse of his never pulled a plow in its life."

"He's *not* hiding out!" Maud muttered indignantly. "He's been to Abilene at least four times. I think he ought to be invited."

Maud's opinion was not asked for. Christmas was to be celebrated without the Southerner.

· 11 ·
Blizzard

THE CHRISTMAS CELEBRATION at the schoolhouse was a
merry success, though Maud's eyes often wandered to
the door, half expecting the Southerner to appear, like
the uninvited bad witch. Then in the excitement of
receiving her gifts and watching Quint and Belle open
theirs, she forgot him.

Quint was pleased and impressed by the shirt she
had made him. Belle pretended to be surprised by her
muffler, though she must have seen Maud knitting it.

Belle's present to Maud *was* a surprise—a dress
length of light-blue calico with white sprigs. How well
it would look with her red hair!

Belle had made Quint a shirt, too. She and Maud
had worked on them together whenever he was out.

Quint had spent a lot of time in the stable, whittling, and he now produced a little box with a carved

top for Belle to keep hairpins in. For Maud he had carved a wooden bowl from a chunk of walnut.

"It's beautiful!" Maud gasped. "Where did you get the wood?"

Quint grinned. "Wes Randolph. I traded an afternoon's work for it one day when you thought I was hunting."

The evening passed with no unexpected incidents.

The new year—1871—brought day after day of bitter cold. The sun shone but gave no warmth. Underfoot the frozen, windswept ground felt like iron. At home and at school Quint wore both new shirts at once. Maud and Belle wore two dresses and wrapped themselves in their shawls, even indoors.

Two things varied the monotony for Maud. Her lessons changed, and sometimes her snares held rabbits or a prairie chicken and sometimes she went home empty-handed and they dined next day on beans and salt pork. All the dried beef had been eaten.

Twice while visiting her snares Maud caught glimpses of the Southerner returning from town. Her curiosity was again aroused. Late one nearly windless afternoon when snow was falling fitfully, she wandered across the prairie to look down into Dry Creek gully and see the dugout. Smoke came from the chimney, so he was home. The open stable had been walled tight with brush leaving only room enough to get the horse in and out. A buffalo hide had been tacked to hang over the doorway.

Quint saw her coming back from that direction, so she had to lie and say she'd forgotten where she placed one of her snares. After that she gave up spying.

Later, at school, Bud reported seeing smoke from the dugout's chimney pipe, so the Southerner was still there. Maud sat on her school bench and dreamed about him. She made up a background of sisters, aunts, and uncles. She gave him a noble reason for leaving home, and a romantic reason for being a loner.

In mid-January, Shorty took to going to town every other week. The hard, frozen ground made the trip an easier one than at other times of the year, though the threat of storm was always there. He stayed overnight at the livery barn and did any errands Belle desired. His trips made a break in the monotony for his children, too. He left them with Belle and Maud, where they got some decently cooked meals. They also got their heads washed with kerosene to kill any lice. Bud shared Quint's bed; Luanne slept between Maud and Belle.

At last, toward the end of February, a break came in the cold weather. For two days the wind blew from the south. The ground thawed on top and turned to mud. Despite the mud, Shorty Haynes went to town.

"Can it be spring?" Belle asked on the way to school the second morning.

Maud sighed. "I wished it was!" She sniffed the air. "I feel a storm coming."

"Says the old Indian!" Quint scoffed.

However, by noon everyone felt the weather changing. The wind stopped. The prairie lay waiting. The air felt sharp and smelled somehow different.

While everyone was playing Skin the Cat, Maud wandered by herself down the wagon track, imagining the thrill of encountering the Southerner, though there wasn't a chance of his riding by this time of day.

Belle called her pupils inside to begin afternoon classes. Maud was the last one in. If she hadn't been last, she might not have seen the cloudbank creeping over the horizon.

As it was, she ran inside and whispered to Belle. Belle watched the cloudbank from the window while the school settled down. Then she rapped her desk with a ruler.

"A storm is coming, children. School's over for today. Get your wraps and put them on quietly."

The younger Martin children looked frightened. Belle smiled at them. "I haven't seen one of your prairie blizzards yet, but I'm told it's best to be home by the fire when they arrive." The little ones looked less alarmed. "Henry, I don't want you setting off alone. Quint, will you go with him? I've heard how quickly these snowstorms come up. I'm not going to take chances. I'll make sure the Martin children get home. Maud, you, Bud and Luanne go straight to our place. Take your books, all of you, so you can study at home. Hurry, now!"

By the time they were ready to leave, the cloudbank was unrolling over the prairie like a dirty featherbed. The icy wind seemed to come straight from the North Pole.

Quint and Henry set off south. "If it's snowing when you get to Martins', stay there," Quint called over his shoulder to Belle. "You know Maud can manage."

His words made Maud feel warm inside even though the biting wind cut through her every layer of clothing as she and the two Haynes children scurried along.

They reached the sod house, and still the snow had not begun to fall. Spot ran to meet them. They burst into the room and closed the door against the blast. The thick sod walls shut out much of the wind's howl.

"Bud, you start the fire," Maud panted. "Make some tea and play with Spot. I'm going to fetch the animals."

Ice was forming on the mud puddles as Maud ran over the frozen prairie to where the cow was staked. But when she came to the place, there was no sign of Lady or the calf. She ran further, knew she'd gone too far, and turned back. It was then she stumbled across the hole where she'd driven the picket pin that morning. Of all the times to be careless! She hadn't driven it deeply enough into the frozen ground. Lady had pulled it up as she grazed and, finding herself free, had probably worked her way down the gradual slope to the creek. With luck, the picket pin would catch in the brush there.

Maud had planned to get Lady first, then hunt for Sam. Now she went to find the horse. Riding him, she'd soon find Lady.

Sam was in the timber, but the coming storm had made him skittish. Maud cornered him between the creek bank and a plum thicket. He broke through the thicket and galloped up the path toward the house and his stable.

"If you think you're getting oats tonight, you're wrong!" Maud screamed after him.

She threw a clod at the thin ice covering the pool and studied the sky. Should she walk all the way to the shed for that pesky horse, or hunt Lady on foot? She decided not to waste time getting the horse. Snowflakes were beginning to fall. With luck she would find Lady and get back to the house before snow hid the path.

In the sparse timber, sheltered from the wind, the snow fell lightly. She saw her cattle at the first bend of the creek. This was Jake's land—not that it mattered.

The picket pin and rope were tangled in an elderberry bush. Twigs caught at Maud's mittens and she had to take them off to work; then the iron pin was so cold she winced every time she had to touch it. It took time and patience to untangle the rope, but at last she freed it. Snow was falling thicker by that time. She wrapped the rope round and round the picket pin so she wouldn't have to touch the iron, and started out.

"Home, Lady!" she shouted. The cow knew what was expected of her and bellowed for her calf. The sound echoed against the clifflike bank on the far side, breaking into the soft whisper of snowflakes. Maud shivered. "Lady, let's go!" she said again, wanting to hear the sound of her own voice in the stillness.

Lady moved off downstream. The calf came galloping, tail high. He was getting big. They would have to decide soon whether to sell him or eat him. With that end in mind, they had never given him a name.

Their progress through the timber was quiet. No fallen branches cracked underfoot; they had all been gathered for kindling.

At the pool Maud turned away from the creek bottom and started up the slope to the prairie. As soon as she left the creek bank, she saw that the screeching wind was blowing the snow straight across the earth. It was a wonder it ever fell to the ground. Her heart thudded, and she suddenly knew what it was to be terrified. Tiny frozen flakes stung her face. She could barely see Lady's rear end. If she hadn't been holding the rope, she would have lost her. The calf had disappeared into the blowing snow, but a bellow from Lady called it to her side.

Nothing in the snow-filled fury showed where the path had been. Through Maud's mittens and the rope around it, the picket pin felt like an icicle. She fought against rising panic. She and Lady would never find the house now. They might walk right past and never see it and go on walking across the empty prairie till they froze to death.

The cow couldn't find her way, either. Cattle tended to drift before the blast. Maud would do better to keep Lady and the calf somewhere nearby, sheltered from the spiteful wind. Maybe they could bed down together against a bank. The cow's warmth would keep Maud warm. Such shelter would be better than wandering the empty prairie.

She tugged at Lady's rope, pulling her back. The cow swung round, head and horns now visible, her rump lost in swirling snow. Cold had already crept through Maud's boots. She tried to recall some sheltered spot along the creek bottom.

The most sheltered spot was Jake's dugout! Did she dare go there? Would Belle be angry if she did? Belle had expressly told her to stay away, but surely that didn't apply in a case like this.

Leading Lady along the creek bank, Maud argued with herself. What if she went, and the Southerner wouldn't let her in? Worse, what if he looked at her like Joe Kackley did, or put his hands on her and tried to kiss her?

In her imagination she had made him somebody special, but she knew well enough that the man in Jake's dugout was not the man of her daydreams. If only he had been invited to the Christmas party! Then she would know what she was getting into. There'd be room in the stable for Lady and the calf. The animals would be welcome because they'd help keep his horse warm.

Maud led the cow steadily through the brush while she built up her courage. She'd rather take a chance with the man than freeze. Even frostbitten fingers and toes were painful. Who knew, perhaps the man had gone to town and she'd find the dugout empty, awaiting her.

She trudged ahead. The cow followed docilely, trusting Maud to lead her to shelter. Maud had no idea exactly how far the dugout was. She had never explored Coddington's part of the creek. Now they were getting into a willow thicket. She turned left and led the cow down into the frozen creek bed.

The mud banks below the steep sides of the ravine were filled with drifting snow. Out of the wind, the ravine seemed almost warm. If worst came to worst, and he wouldn't let her in. . . . No, he'd let her in. The worst would be that he'd be so awful she'd want to leave. In that case, she'd come back to this spot. Proudly she remembered Quint's last words: "You know Maud can manage." Was foisting herself on their unsavory neighbor managing? The thought made her want to giggle.

Careful now, she thought. I must get a sense of the surroundings, or I might pass the dugout.

The cold and the wind would keep her from smelling either manure or woodsmoke. It seemed she had already come a long way, but following a winding creek bank, the way always seemed long.

She tried to walk closer to the steep bank, but it was falling back and widening out. She was crossing a gentle slope—the slope that led to Jake's door?

Searching the fuzzy whiteness, she trudged up the slope. The curtain of gray everywhere behind the snow had grown darker, as though she were in a deep canyon with black walls.

Before she had time to be more frightened, she saw a light—a glowing square of yellow in the snow-filled gloom. She had reached Jake's dooryard! With a gasp of thankfulness, she all but stumbled over the wooden doorstep.

"Hello!" she shouted, pounding on the door. "Mr. Southern!" She hoped that was his name. It didn't matter. The fierce wind whipped her voice away almost before she heard it herself. She pounded with the picket pin. Mr. Southern was home; he would have a fire going. She was safe.

She waited impatiently, stomping her feet. How long did it take to open a door? The man couldn't be asleep—not with the lamp burning!

No matter what, Lady and the calf must be stabled. She couldn't barge into the dugout leading a cow. So why didn't she go to the stable dugout first?

The stable had been built for two horses. There would be room for Lady and the calf, if it didn't kick up its heels.

The buffalo hide that covered the door was pinned back! What did that mean? Had someone knocked the Southerner on the head and stolen the horse? Or had he gone out to find it and bring it in?

A fiercer blast of wind almost blew her through the doorway. Total, warm-smelling darkness engulfed her. She felt the stamp of the horse, startled by her sudden entrance. Good, it was safe, then. The Southerner must simply be asleep. She tugged on Lady's rope to coax her into the strange stable.

A man's voice spoke from the darkness. "Mister, my gun's on you."

Maud jumped. The picket pin fell from her cold fingers and struck her toe. Her cry of fright and her gasp of pain were alike lost in the howl of the wind. What kind of man wore a gun in his own stable? Only an outlaw!

"Who are you?" the voice demanded.

Maud had never been so frightened. "Maud McPherson," she squeaked.

"A girl!" The voice choked with laughter. "Great Heavenly days! I figured you for Jake Coddington." Both laugh and voice sounded friendly. Maud heard herself giggle weakly. Her eyes grew accustomed to the dark. She saw the man standing by the horse's head.

"I couldn't get home—" she was beginning when she felt the picket pin drag over her foot. "My cow!" She sprang to the door in time to see Lady turning away. Dodging a horn she caught the rope close to where it encircled the cow's neck. She turned to find the Southerner behind her.

He said, "Pull her in. I'll twist her head. She'll take the door frame down if she tries to come straight through."

With a quick move, he ducked behind the cow's head and grabbed a horn in each hand.

"She's wild!" Maud screeched above the wind.

However, he knew what he was doing. They said he had come from Texas. In no time Lady was tied to the manger with freedom to lie down. Rough posts between the stalls held up the roof and would keep those wide-branching horns from poking the horse.

"Does she have to be milked?" the Southerner shouted.

"She's drying up," Maud shouted back. Further speech could wait till they could go inside and shut out the howling wind.

Maud stood by while he fastened the buffalo hide so it wouldn't flap open. Then he ushered her into his dugout.

The room was cleaner than Maud would have thought possible. Naturally she had never been inside when the Coddingtons lived there. Someone, surely this man, had whitewashed the dirt walls.

But when she saw her host in the lamplight, she felt misgivings. His black beard did not dismay her. All the men she knew let their whiskers grow. Shaving was too difficult under their primitive living conditions. It was this man's eyes; they were gray and piercing. They saw things about her she didn't know herself. His eyes made her uncomfortable.

He shook snow from his hat and hung it on a peg. The back of the room was stacked from floor to roof with firewood.

"Better shake your shawl," he said mildly.

Maud wasn't ready to remove it, but she couldn't stand around dripping. He took the snowy garment from her shoulders and shook it against the stove. Icy flakes sizzled against the hot iron sides.

"Draw up a keg and sit down," he invited. With a ladle made from a gourd he ladled broth into a teacup.

Maud looked about the small, neat cave. The stacked wood and the bed took up the back half. The little cookstove stood against one wall. Its stovepipe went up through the roof. Grain sacks stood against the other wall. There were two nail kegs for chairs and an upended box for a table. Wooden pegs over the bed held an assortment of objects. Then Maud's attention was riveted to a shelf cleverly hung by ropes from the rafters supporting the dirt roof. The shelf held books—ten, she counted. The postmaster's gossip was true!

She had already noticed that he spoke like someone who'd been to school a lot—like Belle, in fact—except for his soft accent. She began to lose her fear of him.

He sat on the other keg and watched her sip the broth.

"So you're my neighbor," he said. "I believe your land runs next to mine."

His land! Maud gulped and felt broth burn all the way to her stomach. He was calling the place his! She managed to nod.

"That lady who teaches school—is she your sister?"

Maud almost smiled, thrilled to be taken for Belle's sister. "No," she explained. "I just live there. Quint's not related, either. He's from Texas. The herders left him with us when he broke his leg, him and the cow."

The Southerner grinned. "I hope he's as useful as the cow."

"Oh, he is!" Maud opened her mouth to explain how Quint was useful and then closed it again. Better not bring up Jake Coddington.

"Your name's Maud, I believe you said." The man's eyes were sharp. He wasn't the kind of person you'd want to lie to.

"Yes."

"And your friend?"

"Belle. Belle Warren."

"Pretty. So's Maud. And the boy is Quint?"

Maud nodded again.

"What's your name?" she asked at last.

He seemed to hesitate. Then he said, "Call me Tom Southern."

"Mr. Southern," she repeated. She had never heard anybody called Southern. Or Eastern or Northern, for that matter. He hadn't said that was his name: he'd said, "Call me Tom Southern." Maud knew that men sometimes changed their names when they came West.

He was watching her intently, as if he could read her thoughts.

"We heard you came from Texas," she said.

"I think you've guessed I'm a Southerner, not a Texan."

She nodded, quickly turning her eyes to the window behind him, trying not to let them rest on the gray coat he had hung on the door. The pane of glass reflected the lamplight. It was growing dark outside.

"Even though I helped bring cattle from Texas. Aren't Southerners welcome here?"

Was he referring to the Christmas party? Maud felt her face grow hot.

"We though you were a friend of Jake Coddington's," she mumbled. "Until you shot him. Shot *at* him, I mean." His eyes were on her face, waiting for what she would say next. She looked at the toes of her boots. "After that we didn't know what to think."

"What did Coddington tell you?"

Remembering the sight of Jake limping up the track after all his boasting, Maud grinned. "He told us he was going to run you off his claim."

"I had him figured." Tom Southern nodded to himself. "He thought I'd scare easy. Or maybe he thought dead men don't have claims. I won this claim fair in a poker game. I guess I should have spread that around the neighborhood. I'm not bragging about it. But it's legal. He relinquished and I filed."

"You're really fixing to stay here?" Maud couldn't keep the happiness from her voice. Imagine having a neighbor who owned books!

Tom Southern nodded. "I'm ready to settle. This is as good a place as any."

He was quite talkative. Maud was reminded of Mr. Nelson when she first went there to do his chores. Mr. Nelson said he'd been living alone so long he'd gotten out of the habit of talking. Then he limbered up and talked a lot. This man was like that. Due to the storm maybe, he was limbering up faster.

"I've got a bunch of cattle somewhere west of Abilene," he told Maud. "We brought them up from Texas and then couldn't make a sale. Some of the boys took them out west to winter over on the open prairie. They figured on making themselves a dugout. You see, when the owner couldn't sell, he couldn't pay our wages. If I hadn't been lucky in that poker game, I'd have had to go along with them and share their dugout. As it was, I won a place of my own, and a grubstake, too. But I figured Coddington for trouble. I was expecting him to come calling."

"Did you know he twisted his ankle?" Maud asked.

Tom Southern nodded. "I saw him limping. My bullet creased his horse. I sure didn't mean to. I meant to crease him, but the horse swung around."

He got up to lift the kettle lid and poke the meat with his knife. By stretching her neck Maud could see potatoes in the pot, too.

He said, "I guess your friends will be worried. I hear these prairie snowstorms go on for two and three days."

"I'm worried about Belle," Maud exclaimed. "She was taking the Martin kids home first. They live over east. I hope she didn't get caught on the way back. She's new out here." The blizzard itself might frighten Belle. Would Quint keep her spirits up? Maud wished she could be sure.

"Have the Martins been here long?"

"I think they came right after the war."

"They won't let her do anything dangerous." He poked the meat again. "I guess this stuff's ready."

His few dishes were stacked at the back of the table. He removed the cloth that covered them, filled two bowls with stew, and laid out two spoons.

"You don't have a knife," he observed. Using the bowie knife from his belt, he cut the meat in both bowls into bite-sized pieces. The knife was clearly well-sharpened.

"Sorry I don't have forks," he apologized. "A man living alone becomes a barbarian."

Maud nodded. "Mr. Nelson said that, too."

He asked who Mr. Nelson was, but she wasn't ready to tell him everything. "He was a neighbor," she said.

She tasted the steaming stew and burned her tongue. "What meat is that?" she asked.

"Antelope. I shot it south of here last week."

Maud studied the dishes. "Did those come from the Coddingtons?"

"Yes, and were they dirty!"

Maud giggled. "Eph was no housekeeper. Where do you get water? The creek's been awful low."

"There's a pool upstream a ways. As long as this lasts we can melt snow."

He asked who else lived nearby. Maud found herself telling him how Charlie Dexter and Mr. Martin had left to find work, how Shorty Haynes wanted to find a wife to look after Luanne and Bud. Perhaps she was telling too much, but Tom Southern was a good listener. He laughed easily and seemed to find her entertaining. She felt relaxed and warm and well-fed. Before she realized, she was describing Mr. Nelson's death and Belle's arrival, and how she and Belle had become partners.

"She was lucky to find a loyal friend," Tom said. He had told her to call him Tom. He said being called "Mister Southern" made him feel like somebody else.

At last she overcame her shyness enough to say, "You sure have a lot of books! I guess if I hadn't dropped in, you'd have read."

He smiled. "Books aren't the same as company. They talk to you, but you can't talk to them. Do you like to read? Maybe you'd like to read aloud while I wash dishes?"

The idea sounded delightful, but she didn't want to stumble over the words. "I could wash dishes while you read," she suggested.

He laughed. "I won't say no to that!"

He had water and the coffeepot heating on the stove. Maud washed bowls and cups while Tom read from a book called *David Copperfield.* She liked Tom's voice. How funny that she'd thought him frightening! The story was so exciting she began to hope the blizzard would go on till the book was finished.

After a while Tom said his voice was getting tired, so Maud read. After that they took turns, chapter for chapter. Rather than listen with folded hands Maud asked if he had any mending.

Tom grinned. "I'm wearing all my socks at the moment, and my three shirts, too. I'm pretty good at mending. Someone taught me to darn quite well."

"Who?"

He shrugged and poured himself a last cup of coffee. "I've forgotten who."

His words puzzled her, but David Copperfield's adventures soon reclaimed her attention.

They read until Maud's eyes began to close.

"Bedtime!" Tom startled her awake. "You take the bed. I'll spread a buffalo hide on the floor and wrap myself in the other one."

She tried to protest, but he said, "If I sleep on the floor, I'll wake up when the fire dies down and can keep it going."

There was no question of undressing. Maud took off her shoes and crawled between the blankets. Tom spread her shawl over the top. She fell asleep while she was still saying her prayers.

Next morning the blizzard was still screaming. A lot of snow had drifted into the creek bottom. Tom collected bucketfuls to melt for the animals. Maud wanted to help, but he said there was no use in two people getting cold. She could hardly wait for him to finish feeding and watering the animals so they could go on with the story.

For breakfast they ate cornbread and molasses. Maud was enjoying herself, but she wanted to get home, too. Belle and Quint mustn't be kept worrying about her any longer than necessary. From time to time as the day passed, she or Tom scraped the frost from the windowpane so they could look out. Each time nothing was to be seen but whirling snow.

"If all those flakes were to lie still, a man would need snowshoes," Tom remarked. But they both knew the prairie would be cleanswept, the gullies full of drifted snow.

For dinner they ate more stew. After dinner Maud

washed the dishes. When she opened the door to throw out the dishwater, she found she could see the other bank of the creek.

"It's quitting!" she cried.

Tom came to look. "Appears that way. Maybe you'll get home today."

Maud wanted to start immediately, but Tom Southern made her wait till the snow really stopped. It wasn't safe to start out until the sky cleared. Reluctantly she admitted he was right.

Half an hour later a pale, wintry sun slanted into the ravine. The dugout's door and window faced west. The yellow beam sparkling on the frosted window brought them hurrying out. Everything in the creek bottom was mounded and smoothed by glistening snow. The clear blue sky, the yellow light touching the frozen earth of the ravine walls made Maud's heart lift. She sniffed the cold, clean air.

"Brrr!" Tom dove back into the dugout.

While Maud pinned her shawl and put on her mittens, Tom shrugged into his coat.

"I'll saddle Prince and take you home."

Maud protested that she could very well walk the half mile, but Tom said Prince needed exercise. When she was ready, he tossed her up into the saddle.

They made a procession across the prairie. Tom led Prince, Maud rode like a princess. The cow came along at the end of her rope, and the calf kicked up his heels and followed. Maud wished someone would look out and see her triumphal arrival. As they drew near the house, she saw Shorty's horse and wagon standing by the lean-to. He would have set out from town yesterday before the snow started and had probably sheltered overnight at some homestead along the trail. He must have started on home this afternoon as soon as the blizzard began to let up.

Suddenly she forgot her triumph. What if Belle wasn't there?

They entered the yard. She was still atop the high-stepping black horse when Quint flung the door open.

"Here she is!" he shouted to those inside. Belle, Bud, Luanne, and Shorty erupted from the house.

Maud slid from Prince's back, and they surrounded her, hugging her and slapping her shoulders.

"Where have you been?" Belle demanded.

"Mr. Southern took me in!"

"I told you so!" Quint's voice was loud with satisfaction. "Didn't I say that's what she'd do?"

Maud turned to introduce her rescuer.

Belle smiled at him and reached up to smooth her hair. Her cheeks were pink, her eyes sparkling. She looked uncommonly pretty. Tom Southern took off his wide-brimmed leather hat and made a stiff bow. He shook hands with Quint and Shorty. Maud felt he was the best-looking man she'd ever seen. He wasn't finicky, but he had made Maud want to look her best, too. His beard was trimmed, his hair cut, his face clean, and he didn't chew tobacco, so his teeth were nice. In contrast, Shorty Haynes looked like a scruffy dog, his whiskers bristling every which way, his face red and chapped.

Bud and Luanne began firing questions at her, but Shorty said, "Inside, ladies, before you catch cold," and they trooped into the house. Belle found places for everyone to sit, the men on the kegs, the young folks on the bed.

Maud told her story. Tom had little to add. Belle thanked him and smiled upon him. Shorty glared.

"Did *you* get home all right, Belle?" Maud asked.

"Oh, yes," Belle said. "Quint was afraid I'd do something foolish. As soon as he saw Henry to his door, he ran all the way to Martins'—"

"Not *all* the way," Quint disclaimed with a grin that showed his broken tooth. "As much as I could."

"We barely made it," Belle continued. "When you didn't come back, I felt it was my fault for sending you three children alone. But Quint insisted you'd know what to do."

"I was worried, too," Quint whispered. Maud was sitting beside him on the bed. "I'd have gone looking for you if it would have done any good."

"Come on kids, we got to get home," Shorty said. "It'll be dark in another hour. We got lots to do before then." He stood up. "I expect Miss Belle's had her fill of you."

Belle was prompt to say she'd enjoyed Bud's and Luanne's company, they'd helped take her mind off Maud.

"Ready to go, Mr. Southern?" Shorty asked. "We're going the same way." Obviously he didn't mean to leave the field to the other man, but Maud was satisfied. Surely now it would be easy to invite Tom Southern to visit. If he wanted to bring a book to read aloud, so much the better. Belle would be pleased to have such a refined neighbor.

· 12 ·
Coddingtons

"WHAT DID YOU THINK OF HIM?" Maud asked enthusi-
astically as soon as the three of them were alone.

"He seemed all right," Belle answered cautiously.
"How did you pass the time?"

"We read to each other! He does have books! The
postmaster's story was true. We read almost a whole
book, called *David Copperfield.*" Would she ever get a
chance to finish it?

"You mean you didn't find out what he's doing
here?" Quint exclaimed.

"Of course, I found out!" Maud stamped her foot,
suddenly filled with regret. "We should have asked him
to dinner! That darn Shorty had to carry him off."

"That's no way for a lady to talk," Belle chided.

"What did he tell you about himself?" Quint asked
again.

"He won the claim from Jake! In a poker game. But he wasn't surprised when Jake tried to go back on his word."

"So he's a gambler," Belle said. "He looks like one."

"He and some other men came up from Texas with a herd—like Quint. But his outfit couldn't sell their cattle." Maud explained how Tom had won the claim and didn't have to spend the winter looking after the unsold cattle. Then she began at the beginning and told the whole story of how the storm had caught her.

When she finished, they speculated about Tom Southern's background.

"Did he say anything about the army?" Belle wanted to know.

"No . . . he asked if Southerners are welcome here. I said folks held back from being friendly because they thought he was a friend of the Coddingtons. I didn't tell him that after he shot Jake we held off 'cause we thought he was dangerous. I guess he knew that. He says he's fixing to stay."

"If Jake don't come back and shoot him," Quint said.

"*Doesn't* come back," Belle corrected. She looked a little grim, but it might have been the harsh snowy light that made her face look drawn. She sighed. "I wonder how many years it will take to civilize this country."

What made her say that? Maud and Quint raised their eyebrows at each other.

Uneasily Maud ventured to say, "Mr. Southern was civilized."

"Living in a cave is not civilized!" Belle snapped.

Maud dared not argue that the dugout was white-washed and clean.

After supper Maud began at the beginning of the story of David Copperfield and told it to Quint and Belle as best she could, as far as they had read. Belle agreed to invite Tom Southern to Sunday dinner when the weather warmed up, and Maud had to be satisfied with that.

THE WEATHER turned warm the first week in March.

"We've made it through the winter!" Maud exulted.

"Yes," Belle agreed. "Today certainly feels like spring." They were beginning the last week of school.

Maud said, "I bet if we hunted down by the creek for greens this afternoon, we could find enough for supper."

"Ladies shouldn't speak of betting," Belle reminded her. "But, yes, it would be wonderful to have a mess of greens." They were all tired of corn—cornmeal mush for breakfast, cold cornbread for dinner, fried mush or hominy for supper, and more cornbread. The thought of fresh greens and vinegar made Maud's mouth water.

"Anyway, we made it through the winter," she repeated.

The ground thawed, the snow melted, and the black clay soil turned to mud. Walking anywhere—even across the yard to the well—became a terrible effort.

More and more mud clung to Maud's shoes with each step until her feet became almost too heavy to lift. It was impossible to keep from tracking mud onto the carpet. And at the same time Belle suddenly became fussy. She insisted she couldn't invite company until she could take the carpet outside and beat it.

"It'll be muddy all spring!" Maud wailed. "I'll never learn what became of David Copperfield." She tried to get Belle to let her ride over to visit Tom, but Belle wouldn't hear of it. It was one thing, she said, to land at a single man's dwelling in a blizzard; it was quite another to visit him deliberately. If he wanted to be neighborly, he could call on them. He had stopped several times when he was riding into town, but had never stayed long.

New homesteaders were pouring in. "No matter which way I look, I see smoke," Maud remarked. She and Quint were spading and raking the garden. The ending of school had been timed so the pupils could be at home to help with spring planting.

Often the home-seekers stopped to ask the whereabouts of a certain section. Government surveyors had divided the whole state into sections, townships, and ranges. Everyone knew the number of the section where he lived. Most knew the township and range. In a country without roads, hills, or even towns, there was no other way to describe your land.

AT LAST ONE DAY, to oblige Maud, Quint offered to pay Tom Southern a visit. The hens were laying. Belle let

Maud send him three eggs, but she forbade Quint to ask to borrow books.

"Then stare at them hard," Maud coaxed. She was helping Quint catch Sam so he could ride instead of trudging through mud. Quint promised to do his best.

An hour later he came galloping into the yard, whooping like a cowboy. Spot tore out of the shed, barking his head off. Maud and Belle ran to the door.

"I've got a job!" Quint shouted. "We're going after Tom's cattle." He put Sam in the shed and came clumping back. He removed a book from his pocket and presented it to Maud with a bow.

"You got it!" she squealed, hugging him before he could turn away to scrape his boots.

"Tom's going after the cattle the foreman promised him," Quint bubbled. "He wants me to go. He figures it will take a week."

"You don't have a horse," Maud pointed out.

Quint looked nervously at Belle. "Maybe you'd let me take Sam?"

"I suppose you can. . . ." Belle looked doubtfully at Maud.

"What about us?" Maud cried, suddenly angry. She felt Sam was hers; she had been caring for him and driving him longer than either Belle or Quint. "Supposing we have to go to town?" she demanded.

"For what?" Quint asked.

"I don't know—anything!"

"Shorty can get whatever you need."

Maud bit her lip.

"I know you—you just don't want me to take him,"

Quint teased. He turned to Belle. "When we go through town I'll see about selling the calf."

Belle nodded. Last week Quint had discreetly taken Lady to be mated with a bull, and it was time to sell the yearling. But the whole goings-on was a subject that ladies tried not to talk about.

QUINT AND TOM SOUTHERN set off on Saturday morning. Tom had come over the night before to make the final arrangements, and they had all had a pleasant evening together. Belle seemed especially to enjoy it, and Maude hoped it would happen again when the trip was over. With Quint and Sam gone, however, the claim began to seem lonely right away. Maud felt angry at being left behind, and envious of Quint. "I've never been *any*where," she complained.

"You traveled from Kentucky to Kansas," Belle reminded her.

"That doesn't count. I don't remember."

"Try to bear up," Belle advised. "Your life isn't over."

That evening a horseman rode up to the door. Maud went out, expecting to see a stranger. Instead, it was Charlie Dexter, back from his winter sojourn in Iowa. He was leading a packhorse. The packhorse was Sam!

In answer to Maud's eager questions, he shook his head and climbed wearily down. "Don't ask me—It's all here in this letter Quint left for Miss Belle. As long as I was bringing Sam, I put him to use."

They invited him to share their supper. Maud finished putting it on the table. Mystified, Belle began reading the letter.

"Quint sold the calf!" she exclaimed. "No, wait—he's traded the calf for a horse. He's taking the horse and sending Sam home so we can use him to deliver the calf. I never heard of such a thing! What kind of a trade is that?" Looking puzzled and pretty, Belle laid the letter on the table.

Charlie Dexter grinned. "Say, he's some trader! You mean the other party ain't even seen the calf and he's rode off with the horse? Where's he gone?"

"Didn't you see him!" Maud exclaimed.

Charlie slapped his leg and laughed. "No, ma'am! All I did was stop at the livery stable. The liveryman asked me to deliver Sam and the note. Sounds like a good deal. Depending on the horse. Where'd you say Quint's gone?"

In order to explain, they had to tell him all that had happened during the winter. By the time they finished and he told his news, the cold spring twilight had descended.

Charlie got to his feet. "Time I was getting on home," he said. Maud thought of the cold, damp house he'd find, and shivered. She could picture the rusty stove and the mice nests.

"You're welcome to sleep in Quint's bed," Belle offered.

Maud felt proud. Belle was catching on to the way people helped each other out here.

"I might do that," Charlie said. "That way I could get a fresh start tomorrow."

The next day was Sunday. Charlie set off for his claim at sun-up, taking Sam to carry his extra supplies and promising to return him that evening. Belle said he'd better come back for supper. He was prompt to accept.

"If that isn't just like Quint!" Belle said when Charlie had gone. "How do we know they'll think the calf is a fair trade? What if they want the horse back, and here's Quint gone off with it? What if something happens to the calf before we get him delivered? I'm not even sure I want another horse."

"Maybe we could take the calf to town tomorrow?" Maud suggested.

"Let's put it off till Saturday," Belle said. "Maybe Quint will come back early and can deliver it himself."

THE NEXT DAYS brought beautiful spring weather. Overnight the prairie turned green, the wind soft. Maud could think of nothing but Quint, riding freely over the miles of grass.

The worst of the fine weather was that it brought the Coddingtons.

Maud was alone, doing chores, when they came. Belle had gone to close up the schoolhouse. Maud was at the well when they rode up.

Jake rested one arm on the saddle horn. "Howdy."

Maud said howdy.

"What's the squatter doing these days?"

"How should I know?" Maud replied recklessly.

"Hey, now that ain't polite! Didn't that schoolteacher teach you some manners?" Jake's voice was smooth and threatening.

Quint was right to leave me the pistol, Maud thought fiercely. Still, she ought to be able to outwit these two.

"Ain't you going to ask us to set?" Jake goaded.

Thinking quickly, Maud said, "I don't hardly have time. Miss Belle's down sick. With spots. I sent for Doc." Maud threw a quick glance toward the schoolhouse, in plain sight a quarter of a mile across the prairie, *Belle, stay inside,* she urged silently. If only Belle didn't come out and start home!

Behind Jake, Eph was bobbing his head and leering. When Maud looked straight at him, he raised his hat. "She's getting real pretty, Jake," he said. "All that red hair. And I never seen such blue eyes."

"Eph and me's been thinking about you two ladies all winter." Jake winked. "You must have got mighty lonesome . . . all the men gone."

"They weren't all gone," Maud said. "Mr. Southern was here, and Quint."

Jake said, "That's what we come about. Where's Southern now? Don't look like him or his horse has been there lately."

"He heard we was coming and skun out!" Eph chortled.

Jake's eyes bored into Maud's. "You know where he's at?"

Maud could think of no reason not to tell the truth.

"He's gone to pick up cattle. He says the claim belongs to him."

"Hey, hear that?" Eph slapped the saddle with his

hat. His horse shied and he wrenched at the bit. "Stand still, you son-of-a-gun!"

Jake swore under his breath. "Let's see if he still thinks so when he gets back." He wheeled his horse. "Come on, Eph. We're moving in. Let him get *us* out! He even left us supplies."

"Tell Miss Belle to take care," he added cruelly. "Sounds like smallpox."

"Or cholera!" Eph shouted over his shoulder.

Thank goodness she didn't have either! Now that their backs were turned, Maud dared to look toward the schoolhouse. She saw Belle come out and close the door. That was all right, the Coddingtons were riding the other way, toward the dugout. Nevertheless, Maud hurried to the house. Inside she put down the bucket of water. From its hiding place under Quint's mattress, she brought out the pistol. How heavy it was! She needed both hands to hold it steady. She put it back under the mattress and built up the fire.

When Belle came in, Maud reported what Jake Coddington had said. Belle turned white.

"What will happen when Tom comes back?" she whispered.

Her concern seemed excessive. Maud tried to shrug off such worry. "Mr. Southern will contrive to drive out the Coddingtons," she said confidently.

"It's two against one! They could kill him."

"He took care of himself before," Maud reminded her.

"He was inside then! He had some protection, and Jake was alone. Isn't there anything to be done? If the claim is legally his—No, of course, there's nothing. The marshall has his hands full in town. Oh—!" Belle flounced about the room. "Whatever made me agree to stay here, even a year?"

"It doesn't have anything to do with us!" Maud cried.

"It doesn't?" Belle turned on her. "Don't you care that somebody may get killed over eighty acres of sand-burrs and grasshoppers?" She paced the small space between the door and the stove. "I could offer to sell Jake the eighty acres I bought, and relinquish my claim to this eighty. I wonder if he'd settle for that and leave Mr. Southern alone? Oh! There's so much land still unclaimed. Why can't Tom Southern stay out there where his cattle are?"

"You mean, give up our claim?" Maud's lips could hardly form the words.

Belle burst into tears, saying she didn't know what she meant.

The rest of the day their conversation was subdued. Maud wondered if Belle was a lot more interested in Tom than she had let on. Tom had asked a lot of questions about Belle, too.

To Maud's dismay, next morning Belle said she wasn't equal to the job of civilizing the frontier; she didn't care whether it ever became civilized or not.

"You'd give up the claim before the year is over?" Maud felt stunned all over again.

Belle began to talk about taking Maud with her. If she sold the land, they would have enough money to set themselves up in a little house. Belle could teach, and Maud could attend high school.

Maud felt like bursting into tears, but instead she

set her jaw. Clearly something had to be done about the Coddingtons. If it could be done before Tom and Quint came back, nobody would get shot, and Belle would stop talking about leaving.

All morning while Maud went about her chores, her mind turned over ideas. First she considered putting a skunk down the dugout's stovepipe. No, that wasn't practical. She could think of no way to capture a skunk without being overpowered by the smell herself.

She next thought of flooding the dugout with water by damming the creek, but the Coddingtons would see the water rising long before it drove them out. All they'd have to do would be to tear down the dam. Besides, it might take weeks for the water to rise if it didn't rain.

She hadn't frightened them with her talk of smallpox, either. Didn't they know smallpox was catching?

The best way to get them out would be to destroy the dugout. Blow it up! Such a thing had been done. She had heard the story at Kackleys'. A bunch of neighbors had wanted to get rid of a squatter. One man had dropped a wagon thimble filled with gunpowder down the stovepipe. The gunpowder blew the door out and part of the wall. The squatter came tearing out, too. The other men waiting outside had started shooting. The squatter had jumped on his horse and made tracks.

Would Charlie Dexter help? He really didn't have anything against the Coddingtons. They were pigs, but they hadn't done anything to him. He was too peaceable to get involved in another man's fight, especially a man Belle liked. The same went for Shorty Haynes.

But if it was dark, and she started firing the pistol,

who was to know who was pulling the trigger? Pointlessly she wished for Quint. He'd have been delighted to help.

The more she thought about using gunpowder, the better the idea seemed. If the front of the dugout were blown out, they'd have to leave. They might duck into the horse shed, but the front wall was only brush. Bullets would go right through it. Anyhow, the idea was worth a try.

She could buy gunpowder when they took the calf to town. She had a dollar and ten cents. That ought to buy a lot. If Tom and Quint came back before then, she'd suggest they do it. Of course, Tom might not want to blow up his dugout. Come to that, he might not thank Maud for blowing it up, either, but that was a risk she'd have to take. Her way nobody would get hurt, only singed a little. Belle couldn't get upset at that.

ON SATURDAY MORNING events fell out better than Maud could have hoped. Belle woke with a sore throat and what she described as a swimming head. For her to make the long ride into town was out of the question.

"We'll have to put it off," she croaked at breakfast. "I can't send you alone."

"Why not?" Maud cried. Fortune seemed to be favoring her. She determined to make the most of it. For Belle's sake, as well as her own, she must go through with her plan.

Belle was frowning. "A livery barn is no place for a young girl."

"Quint thought it would be all right, or he wouldn't have sent Sam back for us to use," Maud pointed out, trying not to sound like she was arguing.

Belle sipped her coffee and propped her head on her hand. "We must deliver that animal, I suppose. Promise me you won't talk to any strangers?"

Maud promised eagerly.

"What will you do if they don't want the calf after all?" Belle asked.

Maud shrugged. "Bring him back. Quint will have to straighten it out."

Belle closed her eyes. "I'm going back to bed. Please be careful. Deliver the calf and stop at the post office, and come right back."

Maud kept from looking exultant until Belle disappeared behind the curtain. Then, before putting on her shawl, she took the last bit of money she had from its hiding place and slipped it into her high-topped shoe. She had brought Sam from the pasture last night to save time this morning.

"I'm going out to harness up and put a rope on the calf," she called. "I'll come in before I leave."

"We'll get along better this way," she told Sam as she saddled him with Quint's brother's saddle. "Much better. Nobody will see me riding a-straddle. When I get to town, I'll get off and walk."

Maud turned Lady loose for the day and used the picket rope to tie the calf, fastening the other end to the saddle horn. Then she bounced into the house, snatched her sunbonnet and Belle's letters, called goodbye and ran out again. It hadn't occurred to Belle that Maud wouldn't take the wagon, which would have been more ladylike than riding like a cowboy. But not as much fun. . . .

The ride was slow but pleasant. She didn't want to hurry the calf. Green was springing through the mat of last year's pale grass; meadowlarks were singing in every direction. Today she didn't envy Quint. She was taking her own pleasant trip across the wide grassland.

At the livery barn she learned the details of Quint's trade. The horse he'd traded for had been stabled at the barn early in the fall and never called for. "I didn't need another horse!" the liveryman told Maud. "Taking up space, eating his weight in hay and oats. That calf I can put to use. I already have one yearling. I plan to turn them into an ox team. I could rent an ox team twenty times over."

The calf off her hands, Maud tied Sam to the hitching rail outside the livery barn. Lightheartedly she followed the muddy path to Texas Street. Everything was proceeding according to plan.

The town was alive with sounds—the echo of hammering, the steady buzz of a saw. From the railroad tracks came faint shouts and the lowing of cattle. It was a perfect spring day.

At the general store Maud was dismayed to find men already loafing about the pot-bellied stove. Bravely she marched to the counter.

"What can I do for you, young lady?" the storekeeper asked.

"A pound of gunpowder," she said. Her voice seemed to ring in the silence.

The storekeeper looked doubtful. "Ain't you kind of young for that? Who you planning to blow up?"

The men around the stove guffawed.

"Nobody," Maud lied.

"You're the young lady that lives with the lady homesteader," the storekeeper said. "She's a school-teacher, ain't she? What's a schoolteacher need with gunpowder?"

"It's not for her," Maud said desperately, her heart sinking. She should have had a story ready. She should have known grownups would ask questions. "It's for the boy that's staying with us—Quint Farwell."

"All right, let me think about it," the man said. "What else did you come for?"

"Nothing."

"You mean he sent you all the way to town just for gunpowder? You tell him he better buy his own."

Not a sound came from the men around the stove. They had heard every word and were probably grinning.

Maud crept from the store, her face hot with shame.

· 13 ·
The "Wanted" Poster

Maud felt almost too embarrassed to walk down the sidewalk. But she had to go to the post office. The loafers leaning against the front wall took no notice of her. Gratefully she slipped into the bare, mud-tracked little room.

Two women were asking for mail, and more men were standing about, talking to anyone who had time to chat—newcomers asking the whereabouts of unclaimed land.

Maud waited her turn before the window, staring idly at the posters and notices nailed to the board walls. A man came from behind the partition and pinned up a new one:

WANTED
For Train Robbery
TWO CODDINGTON BROTHERS

Maud drew a sharp breath. Her blood seemed to pound in her ears. In a daze she asked for Miss Warren's mail and accepted three letters and a newspaper. Of course the poster didn't mean the Coddingtons she knew. Eph had been in Missouri all winter. Jake had been here. She stopped before it and read the fine print. The descriptions sounded like Jake and Eph, though it gave no first names.

Maud looked about the room with the idea of talking to someone about the notice, but none of the men gave her a glance. The women had gone. She remembered her promise not to speak to strangers. Her chest swelled with excitement. If it really was the Coddingtons, the marshall would want to know! He could put them in jail. When Tom and Quint came back, Jake and Eph would be locked up. Unless a lot of men on the frontier were named Coddington.

Maud felt timid about asking for the marshall's office, but the man she finally approached directed her up the street as though her question was not unusual. He didn't seem interested in why she wanted an officer of the law.

The jail was behind the marshall's office. Maud didn't want to be seen even in that vicinity, but she made herself go.

Only one man was lounging in the room. He said the marshall had gone to Topeka. Maud didn't ask when he would be back. Instead she hurried away. She had decided to take the poster home and show Belle. Belle would know what to do next.

Back at the post office, the room had emptied out. The postmaster was busy sorting mail, his back turned. Maud whipped the sheet from its tacks in one quick motion and slipped it under her shawl. Then she made for the livery stable. The letters fit into the pocket of her dress, but the newspaper stuck out. She slipped the folded poster behind the paper.

Leading Sam, she walked decorously along the edge of the wheel-rutted road past the last house. Luckily Sam was gentle. He stood patiently while Maud got her toe into the stirrup and hauled herself aboard.

The sun had passed its zenith, and Maud felt a pang of hunger. The afternoon was so warm she removed her shawl and tied it about her waist, trying not to think of food. Hunger, and the poster in her pocket, made her want to hurry, but Sam was no trotter. Maybe she shouldn't have taken the poster, but it had seemed the right thing to do—to show it to Belle.

She lounged in the saddle, singing a little tune and reveling in the sweep of the country.

She had traveled about two miles when the wind changed, beginning to blow sharp and cold from the northwest. Lightning streaked through a low bank of dark clouds there, followed by the distant rumble of thunder.

"Oh-oh," she said aloud to Sam, "we're going to get wet." A spring shower wouldn't hurt, but it was dangerous to be out on the prairie during a thunderstorm. She kicked her heels into Sam's ribs. "Hurry a little!"

From the back of a horse, the miles and miles of

rolling land looked perfectly flat, but they weren't. Cutting through the level land were draws: low places deep enough to hide a herd of antelope or a horse and wagon, or—in the old days—Indians. Therefore Maud wasn't surprised when two horsemen came riding out of a draw a mile away.

Then she recognized the horses. It was the Coddingtons, riding into town!

The menace of the storm was forgotten. In a minute she would be alone with the two men. She took a sweeping glance at the prairie. Nothing in sight, not even a cow. How wrong she had been to steal the poster! Her stinging conscience told her they would read the printed accusation right through the cloth of her pocket.

The men gave no sign of recognition until they were close.

"Here's a pretty thing," Eph chortled, as his horse and Jake's closed in on either side of Sam.

How dared anybody as ugly as Eph make fun of her red hair and freckles, Maud thought furiously. But the way he was looking at her scared her. She tried to make Sam keep going, but Jake guessed her intention and grabbed Sam's bridle.

"Don't be in such a hurry, Little Sister," he drawled. "Eph wants to talk to you."

With a touch of the rein Eph made his horse dance in a half-circle and come up beside Sam, facing the same direction. Maud and Sam were trapped between the Coddingtons' horses.

Eph leaned on the saddle horn and grinned at

her. His beard was fuller and more unkempt than ever. His squinty blue eyes looked less empty than she remembered, and meaner.

"I'm fixing to get a wife," he told Maud. "How'd you like to be the lucky lady and keep house for Jake and me?"

Suddenly Maud was more afraid than she'd ever been in her life. Even during the blizzard she'd never felt in such danger.

"No," she whispered. Her tight throat almost made her choke.

"Why not?" Eph's grin was revolting. His teeth were green next to the gums.

On her other side Jake said, "Come for a visit. You might like it better than you think."

"I'm not old enough to get married!" Maud shrank back in the saddle.

"I guess you'll just have to carry her away, Eph." Jake, too, was grinning. "A lady always says no at first."

Maud told herself they were only indulging in the kind of mean teasing they were known for, but today they were carrying it too far.

"Guess I will," Eph said. He made a grab to pull her onto his horse.

"No!" Maud screamed. "Stop it!" She held tight to the saddle and clamped her legs to Sam's sides. The horse tried to back out of the jostling, but Jake kept hold of its bridle.

In the scuffle Eph knocked the mail from Maud's pocket.

"My letters!" Maud cried.

The newspaper fell under the horses' hooves. The letters and the "Wanted" poster hopped in spurts along the track, propelled by the coming storm.

Jake was laughing. "Be a gentleman, Eph. Get them for the lady before you ab-duct her."

"Sure thing." Eph swung down from the saddle and hastened after the white squares. With one tormenter on foot and his horse not blocking the way, Maud would have kicked Sam into a gallop, but Jake still held Sam's bridle.

The single sheet of paper, being lightest, blew furthest away. Eph captured it last. As he came walking back, he glanced at it and stiffened.

"Stop reading and come on!" Jake snarled, but Eph's attention was all for the paper in his hand.

"Jake, look!" Eph's face had become serious. His eyes were frightened as he handed Jake the "Wanted" poster. "They know it was us." His voice was a hoarse croak.

"What are you talking about?" Jake reached for the poster, looked at it and swore. In a rage he turned to Maud. "Where'd you get this lie?" he shouted.

His raised voice startled his mount. The animal snorted and sidled, tossing its head. Needing both hands to control his own horse, he let go of Sam's bridle.

Maud wasted not an instant. With both heels she kicked Sam as hard as she could and screeched like a Comanche. Whether it was the kick or the yell, or the freedom from the strange hand on his bridle, Sam sprang forward. He set off down the track at a run.

Maud's heart jumped into her throat. She was mad to challenge them like this. Sam was no racehorse. He'd done nothing all winter but eat and grow fat. If they came after her— What would they do when they caught her?

For the first quarter-mile Sam galloped wildly. Then he began to tire. Maud listened for hooves pounding behind her, expecting to be overtaken at any moment. How close were they?

The wagon track dipped into a shallow draw. Coming up out of it, Sam's stride faltered. The road leveled out. Maud dared a look over her shoulder. The Coddingtons were nowhere in sight!

She pulled Sam to a stop. "Whoa, boy, whoa!" Turning in the saddle, she scanned the prairie between her and the town. The men were nowhere to be seen!

She started Sam on, urging him to a steady trot, while she pondered. If the poster had been about them, they would be crazy to waste time chasing her, or going into Abilene, either. If they were smart, they'd get their bedrolls from the dugout after dark, and head for Texas.

Maud remembered they had Belle's letters. Too bad. They would read them, of course, and then throw them away.

As Sam jogged on, however, Maud's fright turned to elation. Maybe the poster would be as effective as gunpowder! Though not as exciting. She had looked forward to the explosion. However, this would save destroying the dugout. She could hardly wait to get home and report. Belle would send Quint to Abilene to tell the marshall, and all might be well.

The rain caught her while she still had a long way to go. She guided Sam into a washout, climbed down from his back, and held him close beside the dirt bank till the worst of the lightning was over. They rode on home in a cold, steady rain.

The first thing she saw when she rode up to the house were two horses in the stable. Her heart thudded. For an instant she thought the Coddingtons had beat her home. Then she recognized the black—Tom Southern's. The other must be Quint's!

Sure enough, hearing her ride up, Quint opened the door of the soddy.

"Howdy, Maud. Food's on the table. Put Sam in. I'll unsaddle him later."

But this Maud was unwilling to do. Poor Sam had had a long day. He was wet and hungry. And Maud was feeling suddenly shy. Quint had been gone only a few days, but in that time she seemed to have grown a lot older. She chuckled. She'd even had a proposal of marriage! Ugh! She wasn't going to tell anyone that. Quint would never stop teasing her.

He might be a tease, but he came into the shed and helped rub down Sam.

"Miss Belle ordered the biscuits to wait," he said with a twinkle, knowing the mention of biscuits instead of cornbread would give her a burst of speed.

"She must feel better," Maud said. "She was sick when I left."

"I guess Tom and me had a good effect on her." Quint was grinning.

"What do you mean?"

"Nothing. She was just glad to see us. She seems real upset about the Coddingtons."

"When did you get here?" Maud asked.

"A little while ago. We turned the cattle loose down on the creek. Tom got fifty head. Most of the herd didn't make it through the winter. They divided up what was left."

When Maud entered the house, Tom Southern stood up, as though she were a grown-up lady. She gave him her best smile, happy at the thought of the good news she had to tell. Belle made her change to dry clothes, and at last they sat down to the meal.

While they ate, Maud told what had happened to her, except the part about trying to buy gunpowder. As she described the poster, Belle's downcast face became brighter. Her look turned to one of shock and worry when Maud began to tell of meeting the Coddingtons.

"What will they do now?" Belle asked Tom when Maud had ended her story.

"If they have any sense, they'll keep riding."

"Do you really think so?"

Tom nodded. "The country's filling up. Last fall when we drove those cattle out there, it was all open range. This spring about everywhere you looked someone was plowing."

Belle nodded thoughtfully.

Quint said, "Speaking of plowing, now we've got a team I could start plowing where the sod's been broken."

"I suppose you could," Belle said.

Maud sucked in a deep breath and then let it out in a whoosh. She looked at Quint with shining eyes, but

he didn't know what had pleased her. He didn't know
about the year. And now it looked as if Belle would
stay on.

"Speaking of horses," Belle began, "tell us how you
worked that deal—trading a calf for a horse. I've heard
of buying a pig in a poke, but I never heard of riding
off on your half of the bargain before the other fellow's
even seen his half."

Tom laughed. "He did it! I was there. That kind
of talent is wasted on a farm."

Quint grinned self-consciously. "I don't know. I
kind of take to farming. Cows, a few pigs, maybe some
sheep."

"Sure thing," Tom agreed. "Something to trade
with."

Quint laughed. "I guess that would be the idea."
He turned to Maud. "Want to see Tom's critters?"

Maud opened her mouth to ask why she should
want to see a bunch of skinny longhorns, but Quint
gave her a meaning wink.

Puzzled, she said, "All right." She borrowed Belle's
dry shawl and followed Quint outside.

As soon as the door was closed, she said, "What
were you trying to tell me?"

"I didn't want to tell you anything. I wanted to
leave Tom and Miss Belle alone."

"Why?"

"Why! Why do you think?"

Maud thought. "Oh," she said finally.

Quint said, "He talked about her darn near the
whole trip. I think she's sweet on him, too."

Maud nodded. "She sure was worried when the

Coddingtons came back. She was afraid they'd fight. I thought she was going to give up and go back East." A great joy filled Maud's chest. "I guess she'll want to stay now."

Quint nodded. "I guess she will."

"They might even get married," Maud suggested.

Quint nodded again. He'd been thinking the same thing because he said, "If they do, I'm going to see about moving into the dugout. Tom's going to need me to help him."

Belle wouldn't have time to teach school if she got married. But a man like Tom would make ends meet. He'd trade work and get the sod plowed, unless he decided to raise cattle. Maud thought she wouldn't be surprised if Tom turned out to be as big a rancher as Mr. Randolph. At any rate, it didn't look like either Tom or Belle would be pulling up their claim stakes and leaving.

Maud gasped. "Maybe Belle won't need me!"

Quint was looking at her almost fondly. "Of course she'll need you." He reached for her pigtail, but she jerked her head away. "Her year of mourning won't be up for months yet."

Maud hardly heard him. She had glimpsed an astonishing truth: Belle had needed her more than she had needed Belle. If Belle had not taken up the claim, Maud could have gone to Abilene as a hired girl. I'm like Quint, she said to herself with sudden satisfaction. We're both orphans. I can look after myself, too. I did all right with the Coddingtons.

The thought of the Coddingtons gone from the dugout and gone from the country gave her the urge to fling up her arms and run. She bounded down the long slope to the creek, forgetting she was too old for such behavior. Quint was thinking of moving into the dugout! That meant he was planning to stay, too!

She heard him thudding behind her. They pulled up at the pool, breathless and laughing. The afternoon shadows were growing long, the spring air was cold.

"I guess that'll make us brother and sister," Quint said, his voice serious.

"How can it?" Maud asked sharply. "Belle's not my sister! And Tom's not your brother!"

Quint was laughing at her. He caught her pigtail this time and pulled it. Her face grew warm. For a moment she thought he might kiss her. But his face turned red, and he stalked off up the creek. "Come on, if you want to see these critters."

Following him, Maud thought, I've got everything I always wanted! Nice people to live with, and a proper home. We'll be able to win this land—I know we will!

She began to run to catch up. "Quint!" she called. "Quint, I'm so happy!"